A Texas Cowboy's Christmas

CATHY GILLEN THACKER

MILLS & BOON®

First Published in Great Britain 2016
By Mills & Boon, an imprint of HarperCollins Publishers
1 London Bridge Street, London, SE1 9GF

Large Print edition 2016

© 2016 Cathy Gillen Thacker

ISBN: 978-0-263-06621-0

Our policy is to use papers that are natural, renewable and recyclable products and made from wood grown in sustainable forests. The logging and manufacturing processes conform to the legal environmental regulations of the country of origin.

Printed and bound in Great Britain
by CPI Antony Rowe, Chippenham, Wiltshire

Cathy Gillen Thacker is married and a mother of three. She and her husband spent eighteen years in Texas and now reside in North Carolina. Her mysteries, romantic comedies and heartwarming family stories have made numerous appearances on bestseller lists, but her best reward, she says, is knowing one of her books made someone's day a little brighter. A popular Mills & Boon author for many years, she loves telling passionate stories with happy endings and thinks nothing beats a good romance and a hot cup of tea! You can visit Cathy's website, cathygillenthacker.com, for more information on her upcoming and previously published books, recipes and a list of her favorite things.

Chapter One

"I blame *you* for this, Chance Lockhart!" Molly Griffith fumed the moment she came toe-to-toe with him just inside the open-air bucking-bull training facility of Bullhaven Ranch.

Chance set down the saddle and blanket he'd been carrying. With a wicked grin, he pushed the brim of his hat back and paused to take her in. No doubt about it—the twenty-seven-year-old general contractor/interior designer was never lovelier than when she was in a temper. With her amber eyes blazing, her pretty face flushed with indignant color and her auburn curls wildly out of place, she looked as if she were ripe for taming.

Luckily for both of them, he was too smart to succumb to the challenge.

His gaze drifted over her, taking in her designer jeans and peacock-blue boots, before moving upward to the white silk shirt and soft suede blazer that cloaked her curvy frame.

Damn, she was sexy, though. From the half-moon pendant that nestled in the hollow of her breasts to the voluptuous bounty of her bow-shaped lips.

Exhaling slowly, he tamped down his desire and prompted in a lazy drawl, "Blame me for what?"

Molly propped her hands on her hips. "For telling my son, Braden, he can have a live bull for Christmas!"

Somehow Chance managed not to wince at the huffy accusation. He set down the saddle and narrowed his eyes instead. "That's not *exactly* what I said."

Molly moved close enough he could inhale her flowery perfume, her breasts rising and falling with every deep, agitated breath. "Did you or did you not tell him that Santa could bring him a bull?"

Chance shrugged, glad for the brisk November breeze blowing over them. Still holding Molly's eyes, he rocked back on the heels of his worn leather work boots. "I said he could *ask* Santa for a bull."

Molly harrumphed and folded her arms beneath her breasts, the action plumping them up all the more. "Exactly!"

Working to slow his rising pulse, Chance lowered his face to hers and explained tautly, "That doesn't mean Santa is going to *bring* it."

Chance picked up the gear, slung it over one shoulder and stalked toward the ten-by-ten metal holding pen, where a two-year-old Black Angus bull named Peppermint was waiting.

One of the heirs to his retired national championship bucking bull, Mistletoe, he bore the same steady temperament, lively personality and exceptional athletic ability of his daddy.

After easing open the gate, Chance stepped inside.

Aware Molly was still watching his every move, he proceeded to pet the young bull in training. Once gentled, he set the saddle on Peppermint's back.

Swallowing nervously at the thousand-pound bull, Molly stepped back. With an indignant toss of her head, she continued her emotional tirade. "You really don't have a clue how all this works, do you?"

Chance sighed as he tightened the cinch and led Peppermint into the practice chute, closing the gate behind him. "I have a feeling you're about to tell me."

Molly watched him climb the side rails and secure a dummy on the saddle via electronically controlled buckles.

Feeling the unwelcome extra weight, Peppermint began to snort and paw the ground within the confines of the chute.

Even though she was in no danger, Molly retreated even farther. "A child writes a letter to Santa, asking for his most precious gift. Then Santa brings it."

Chance plucked the remote control out of his pocket. "That wasn't how it worked in my home." He signaled to his hired hand Billy to take his position at the exit gate on the other side of the practice ring. "I remember asking Santa for a rodeo for my backyard in Dallas. Guess what?" He shot her a provoking look that started at her face and moved languidly over her voluptuous body before returning to her eyes. "It didn't happen."

Molly rolled her eyes, still staying clear of the snorting, increasingly impatient Peppermint. Digging her boots into the ground, she fired back, "I cannot help it if your mother and father did not appropriately censure your wishes in advance."

Chance hit the control. Immediately, the sound of a rodeo crowd filled the practice arena. He released the gate, and Peppermint, tired of confinement, went barreling into the ring.

For the next few seconds, he bucked hard to the right and came down. Went up and down in the middle, then bucked to the left.

And still the crowd sounds filled the air.

Adding to the excitement, as Peppermint bucked higher and higher…and seeing the kind of athletic movement he wanted, Chance rewarded the bull with the release of the dummy.

It went flying. And landed facedown in the dirt.

Billy whistled.

Peppermint turned and followed the waving Billy out the exit gate and into another pen, where he would receive a treat for his performance.

Chance cut the crowd sounds on the intercom

system. Silence fell in the arena once again, and Chance lifted a hand. "Thanks, Billy!"

"No problem, boss!" he replied before going off to see to the bucking bull.

Molly said, looking impressed despite herself, "Is that how you train them?"

"Yep."

"Too bad no one can train you."

"Really? That's juvenile, even for you, Molly."

He knew where it came from, though. She brought out the irascible teenager in him, too.

Chance went back into the barn, checking on his thirty bucking bulls, safely ensconced in their individual ten-by-ten metal pens, then took a visual of those in the pastures. Finished, he strode across the barnyard to a smaller facility, where his national champion was kept.

Mistletoe's private quarters, his ranch office, veterinary exam, lab and breeding chute, and equipment facility were all there. All were state-of-the-art and a testament to what he had built.

"Look, I'm sorry," Molly said, dogging his

every step. "But I'm trying to help my son be realistic here."

Chance paused to pet Mistletoe. The big bucking bull had a little gray on his face these days, but he was still pleasant as ever to be around. "Is that what you're doing for Braden?" He gave his beloved Black Angus one last rub before turning back to Molly. "Helping him temper his expectations? Or censuring all his dreams?"

Molly muttered something he was just as glad not to be able to understand, then threw up her hands in exasperation.

"I want my little boy to grow up being practical!"

Chance spun around, and she followed him back down the center aisle. "Unlike certain idiot cowboys who shall remain nameless."

There she went with the insults again, but it was better than dealing with the smoldering attraction they felt whenever they were together.

Chance paused at the sink in the tack room

to wash and dry his hands, then walked out to join her. Saw her shiver in the brisk, wintry air.

Aware the day looked a lot warmer than it actually was, he turned away from the evidence of her chill and drawled, "I think I *might* know who you're talking about." Rubbing his jaw in a parody of thoughtfulness, he stepped purposefully into her personal space.

Watching her amber eyes widen, he continued, "That rancher brother of mine, Wyatt, down the road. None too bright, is he?"

Molly made a strangled sound deep in her throat. Rather than step away, she put her hand on the center of his chest and gave him a small, equally purposeful shove. "I'm talking about you, you big lug."

Delighted by her unwillingness to give any ground to him, he captured her hand before she could snatch it away and held it over his heart. "Ah. Endearments." He sighed with comically exaggerated dreaminess.

Temper spiking even more, she tried, unsuccessfully, to extricate her fingers from his. "You're playing with fire here, cowboy."

So he was. But then he had to do something with all the aggravation she caused him. And had been causing, if truth be known, for quite some time.

He let his grin widen, surveying her indignant expression. Dropping his head, he taunted softly, "The kind of fire that leads to a kiss?"

"The kind that leads to me hauling off and kicking you right in the shin!"

It was good to know he could get to her this much. Because she sure got to him. The pressure building at the front of his jeans told him that.

He lowered his lips to hers. "Didn't your parents ever tell you that you can catch more flies with sugar than spite?"

Abruptly Molly's face paled.

Too late, he realized he should have bothered to find out what kind of life she'd had as a kid before hurling that particular insult.

She drew a deep breath. Serious now. Subdued.

Aware he'd hurt her—without meaning to—he let her hand go.

She stepped back. Regaining her composure, she lifted her chin and said in a solemn tone, "I want you to talk to Braden. Tell him you were wrong. Santa doesn't bring little boys live bulls."

At that particular moment, he thought he would do just about anything for her. Probably would have, if she hadn't been so socially and monetarily ambitious and so out of touch regarding what really mattered in life, same as his ex.

But Molly was. So…

Exploring their attraction would lead only to misery.

For all their sakes, Chance put up the usual barbed wire around his heart. "Why can't you tell him?" he asked with an indifferent shrug. "You're Braden's momma, after all." And, from all he'd seen, misguided goals aside, a damn good one.

Molly's lower lip trembled, and she threw up

her hands in frustration. "I have told him! He won't believe me. Braden says that you're the cowboy, and you know everything, and you said it was okay. And that's what he wants me to write in his letter to Santa, and I cannot let him ask Saint Nick for that, only to have his little heart broken."

She had a point about that, Chance realized guiltily. He'd hate to see the little tyke, who also happened to be the spitting image of his mother, disappointed.

Sobering, he asked, "What *do* you want Braden to have?"

Molly's features softened in relief. "The Leo and Lizzie World Adventure wooden train set." She pulled a magazine article out of her back pocket that listed the toy as the most wanted preschool-age present for the holiday that year. Featuring train characters from a popular animated kids' television show, the starter set was extremely elaborate. Which was no surprise.

Since Molly Griffith was known for her big ambitions and even more expensive tastes.

It made sense she would want the same for her only child.

Even if Braden would be happier playing with a plastic toy bull. Or horse…

Sensing she wanted his approval, Chance shrugged. Wary of hurting her feelings—again—he mumbled, "Looks nice."

As if sensing his attitude was not quite genuine, she frowned. "It will bring Braden hours of fun."

Enough to justify the cost? he wondered, noting the small wooden pieces were ridiculously overpriced—even if they were in high demand. He squinted at her. "Are you sure you don't work for the toy company?"

She scowled at his joke but came persuasively closer, even more serious now. "Please, Chance. I'm begging you."

This is new, Chance thought, surprised.

He actually kind of liked her coming to him for help.

She spread her hands wide, turning on the full wattage of maternal charm. "Braden just turned three years old. It's the first Christmas holiday he's likely to ever remember. I really want it to be special." She paused and took a deep breath that lifted the lush softness of her breasts. "You have to help me talk sense into my son."

FOR A BRIEF MOMENT, Molly thought she had finally gotten through to the impossibly handsome cowboy.

Then he folded his brawny arms across his broad chest and let out a sigh that reverberated through his six-foot-three-inch frame. Intuitive hazel eyes lassoed hers. "I want to help you."

Pulse racing, Molly watched as he swept off his black Stetson and shoved a hand through the rumpled strands of his thick chestnut-colored hair. "But?"

Frowning, he settled his hat squarely on his

head. "I can't do to your son what my parents did to me."

"And what was that?" she asked curiously.

"Try and censor and mold his dreams—to suit your wishes instead of Braden's."

Had Lucille and the late Frank Lockhart done that to Chance? The grim set of his lips seemed to say so. But that had nothing to do with her or Braden.

Molly stepped closer, invading his space. With a huff, she planted both hands on her waist and accused, "You just started this calamity to get under my skin."

His sexy grin widened. "I was already under your skin," he reminded her, tilting his head to one side.

True, unfortunately. Molly did her best to stifle a sigh while still stubbornly holding her ground. She wished he didn't radiate such endless masculine energy or look so ruggedly fit in his gray plaid flannel shirt and jeans. Never mind have such a sexy smile and firm, sensual lips…

She could barely look at him and not wonder what it would be like to kiss him.

Just as an experiment, of course.

"So you're really not going to help me?"

Chance's brow lifted. "Convince him he doesn't want to be a cowboy when he grows up? And have a ranch like mine that has all bulls on it? Or get a head start on it by getting his first livestock now?" His provoking grin widened. "No. I'm not going to do any of that. I will, however, try to talk him into getting a baby calf. Since females are a lot more docile than males."

"Ha-ha."

"I wasn't talking about you," he claimed with choirboy innocence.

Yeah…right. When they were together like this, *everything* was about the two of them.

Molly shut her eyes briefly and rubbed at the tension in her temples. With effort, she forced her attention back to her child's fervent wish to be a rancher, just like "Cowboy Chance." Who was, admittedly, the most heroic-looking figure her son had ever had occasion to meet.

Trying not to think about what a dashing figure he cut, Molly turned her glance toward the storm clouds building on the horizon. It wasn't supposed to rain for another day or two, but it looked like it now. "I live in town, remember? I don't have any place to keep a baby calf."

Chance shrugged. "So ask my mother to pasture it at the Circle H Ranch. You're there enough anyway."

Molly wheeled around and headed back to the driveway next to the log-cabin-style Bullhaven ranch house, where she had parked her sporty red SUV. "Even if that were a plausible solution, which it's not, Braden and I aren't going to be here past the first week of January."

Squinting curiously, he matched his strides to hers. "How come?"

Trying not to notice how he towered over her, or how much she liked it, Molly fished her keys out of her jacket pocket. "Not that it's any of your business, but we're moving to Dallas."

Chance paused next to her vehicle. "To be closer to Braden's daddy?"

Her heart panged in her chest. If only her little boy had a father who wanted his child in his life. But he didn't, so...

There was no way she was talking to Chance Lockhart about the most humiliating mistake she'd ever made. Or the fact that her ill-conceived liaison had unexpectedly led to the best thing in her life, a family of her very own. Molly hit the button on the keypad and heard the click of the driver-side lock releasing. "No."

"No, that's not why you're moving?"

He came close enough she could smell the soap and sun and man fragrance of his skin.

Awareness shimmered inside her.

He watched her open the door. "Or no, that's not what you want—to be closer to your ex?"

Heavens, the man was annoying!

Figuring this was the time to go on record

with her goals—and hence vanquish his mistaken notions about her once and for all—Molly lifted her gaze to his. "What I want is for my son to grow up with all the advantages I never had." Braden, unlike her, would want for nothing.

Except maybe a daddy in his life.

Not that she could fix that.

Chance's lip curled in contempt. "Ah, yes, back to social climbing."

He wasn't the only one who misinterpreted the reason behind her quest to get an in with every mover and shaker in the area. And beyond...

But for some reason, Chance Lockhart's contempt rankled.

Which was another reason to set him—and everyone else in Laramie County who misread her—straight. "Look, I don't expect you to understand. You having grown up with a silver spur in your mouth and all."

He grinned.

"But not all of us have had those advantages."

His hazel eyes sparkled, the way they always did when he got under her skin. "Like?"

"Private school, for one."

Chance remained implacable. "They have private schools in Laramie County."

"Not like the ones in Dallas."

He squinted in disapproval. "Which is where you want him to go."

Stubbornly, Molly held her ground. "If Braden attends the right preschool, he can get into the right elementary, then middle, then prep. From there, go on to an elite college."

Chance poked the brim of his hat up with one finger. "I'm guessing you aren't talking about anything in the University of Texas system."

Molly studied the frayed collar on Chance's flannel shirt, the snug worn jeans and run-of-the-mill leather belt. It was clear he didn't care about appearances. Coming from his background, he did not have to. "If Braden goes to an Ivy League school, the world is his oyster."

Chance rested his brawny forearm on the

roof of her SUV. "I can see you've got it all mapped out."

Molly tried not to notice how well he filled out his ranching clothes. "Yes, unlike you, Braden is going to take advantage of all the opportunities I plan to see come his way."

"How does Braden feel about all this?" Chance asked, not bothering to hide his frustration with her.

Had Molly not known better, she would have thought that the irascible cowboy did not want her to leave Laramie County. But that was ridiculous. The two of them couldn't get gas at the same filling station at the same time without getting into a heated argument. More likely, Chance would be delighted to see her depart. "My son is *three*."

"Meaning you haven't told him."

"He has no concept of time."

"So, in other words, no."

"I will, once Christmas is over," Molly maintained. She moved as if to get in her vehicle, but

Chance remained where he was, his big, imposing body blocking the way.

"Has it occurred to you that you're getting ahead of yourself with all your plans to better educate and monetarily and socially provide for your son?"

Chance wasn't the first to tell her so.

She hadn't listened to anyone else.

And she wasn't about to listen to him, either.

Ducking beneath his outstretched arm, she slid behind the steering wheel. Bending her head, she put the key in the ignition. "What I think is that one day, my son will be very grateful to me for doing all that I can to ensure his dreams come true," she retorted defensively.

Chance leaned down so they were face-to-face. "Except, of course, ones that have to do with livestock."

What is it about this man? Molly fumed inwardly. He not only provoked her constantly—he had the potential to derail her at every turn, just by existing!

Pretending his attempts to delay her so they could continue their argument were not bothering her in the least, Molly flashed a confident smile. "You're right," she admitted with a sugary-sweet attitude even he would have to find laudable. "I have gotten way, way off track."

He chuckled. "Back to train analogies?"

She gave him a quelling look.

He lifted an exaggeratedly apologetic hand. "I know. Even some of us big, dumb cowpokes who passed on Ivy League educations know a few big words."

She'd heard Chance had been just as much of a problem to his wealthy parents growing up as he was to her now. "How about 'aggravate'?" She looked him square in the eye. "Do you know what that means?"

He grinned. "I think that's what I do to you, on a daily, hourly, basis?"

So true. Molly drew a calming breath. She started the ignition, then motioned for him to step away. When he did, she put her window down. "I'm going to be at the Circle H this afternoon, meeting with your mother about the proposed kitchen renovation."

"Well, what do you know," he rumbled with a maddeningly affable shrug. "I will be, too."

She ignored the fact that their two contracting companies were competing for the renovation job. "Braden will be with me. It's your chance to make things right with my son. Please, Chance." She paused to let her words sink in. "Don't let us down."

IF MOLLY HADN'T framed it quite like that, maybe he could have bailed. But she had, so at five past three Chance found himself driving up the lane to the Circle H ranch house.

Molly's SUV was already on-site. She and her son, Braden, were by the pasture, where a one-week-old Black Angus was pastured with his momma. Little arms on the middle rung of the fence, Braden was staring, mesmerized, at the sight of the nursing bull.

"Can I pet him?" Braden asked as Chance strolled up to join them.

Her pretty face pinched with tension, Molly shook her head.

Chance hunkered down beside Braden. The little tyke had the same curly red hair, cute-as-a-button features and amber eyes as his mother. "Petting the bull would scare it, buddy, and we don't want that, do we?"

Balking, Braden bartered, "I know gentle. Mommy showed me." Realizing Chance didn't quite understand what he was saying, Braden continued with a demonstration of easy petting. "Kitty cat—gentle. Puppy—gentle. Babies—gentle."

"Ah. You're very gentle with all of those things," Chance concluded.

Braden nodded importantly. "Mommy showed me."

"Well, listen, buckaroo," Chance continued, still hunkered down so he and Braden were eye to eye. "It's always good to be gentle," he said kindly. "And it's great to be able to see a real baby bull."

Braden beamed. "I like bulls!"

"The thing is, Santa doesn't really have any bulls to bring to little boys," Chance told him, quashing the kid's dreams against his better judgment.

"Uh-huh! At the North Pole," Braden said. "Santa has everything!"

"No." Chance shook his head sadly but firmly. He looked the little boy in the eye. "There aren't any bulls at the North Pole."

Mutinously, Braden folded his little arms across his chest. "Santa bring me one," he reiterated stubbornly.

Out of the corner of Chance's eye, he saw Molly's stricken expression. Yeah. She pretty much wanted to let him have it. Given the unforeseen way things were developing, he could hardly blame her.

"For Christmas," Braden added for good measure, in case either Molly or Chance didn't understand him. He pointed to the pasture. "Want mommy bull. And baby bull."

Okay, this was not going according to plan, Chance thought uncomfortably.

"Baby needs mommy," Braden added plaintively, just in case they still weren't getting it.

Molly lifted a brow and sent Chance an even more withering glare.

Fortunately, at that moment, his mother walked out of the recently renovated Circle H bunkhouse, where she was currently living, her part-time cook and housekeeper, Maria Gonzales, at her side. The young woman often brought her own three-year-old daughter, Tessie, to work with her. The little lass peeked at Braden from behind her mother's skirt.

"Braden, Maria and Tessie were just about to make some Thanksgiving tarts. Would you like to help them?" Lucille asked.

He looked at his mother for permission.

Molly gave it with a nod, then pointed to the ranch house on the other side of the barns. "Miss

Lucille, Chance and I are going to walk over there and have a meeting. Then I'll come back to get you. Okay?"

Braden took Maria's outstretched hand. "'Kay, Mommy."

Maria and her two young charges set off.

In the past, the sixty-eight-year-old Lucille had ignored interpersonal tensions for the sake of peace. However, a recent series of life-changing events had caused Chance's mother to rethink the idea of sugarcoating anything. And now, to everyone's surprise, it turned out she could be as blunt as Chance's older brother, Garrett.

"What's going on between you two?" Lucille demanded as she looked from Molly to Chance and back again. "And don't tell me nothing, because I can feel the mutual aggravation simmering between you a mile away!"

Chance would have preferred to keep their tiff private. Unfortunately, Molly had other ideas. "Chance told Braden that he could ask Santa to bring him a real live baby bull for Christmas!" she sputtered.

Lucille turned to him, formidable as always in an ultrasuede sheath, cashmere cardigan and heels.

"I was trying not to quash his dreams," Chance insisted hotly.

"So, instead, you lit fire to impossible ones, and now he wants not just a baby bull but a bovine mama to go with it, too," Molly accused him, looking furious enough to burst into tears.

"Look, I—" Even as the words came out of his mouth, Chance had to wonder how Molly had managed to put him on the defensive.

She stomped closer and waved a finger beneath his nose. "If you hadn't brought that baby bull over with his momma to pasture at the Circle H—"

"If you hadn't brought your son with you to discuss making a bid," he volleyed right back.

Molly planted both her hands on her slender hips. "I had no choice!"

He mocked her by doing the same. "Well, neither did I!"

Completely exasperated, Lucille stopped worrying the pearls around her neck and stepped in between them. "Enough, you two!" she chastised. "You are acting like ornery children. It's five weeks until Christmas...we will figure out a way to work this out."

Chance and Molly separated once again.

Satisfied things were calmer, at least for the moment, Lucille walked up the steps to the rambling, homestead-style ranch house and across the spacious front porch. "In the meantime, I have a job big enough for the two of you," she said over her shoulder, leading the way into the house.

Chance and his crew had spent the fall getting the two bedrooms and bathroom upstairs remodeled, the staircase rebuilt and all new energy-efficient windows installed. A new roof and fiber-cement siding had been put on, and the exterior had been painted a dazzling white with pine-green shutters. They'd also followed the plans of the structural engineer and gutted the downstairs into an open living-kitchen-dining area, a laundry room and mudroom, and what would one day be a spacious master suite with luxury bath for Lucille.

For the moment, however, only the framework of the redesigned first-floor rooms and the original wood floors—which were in need of refinishing—stood.

In the center of the space, in front of the original limestone fireplace, were two big easels. One held Molly's proposed design, the other Chance's.

Lucille turned to her son. "Although I love the rustic nature of your plans, honey, I am going to go with Molly's vision for the first floor."

There wasn't a lot of difference in the plan for the master suite, since Lucille had been very specific in what kind of fixtures and the size closet she wanted. As for the rest…

"You know that's going to cost you twice what mine would," Chance pointed out.

Lucille nodded. "True. But your vision for the space is so...utilitarian."

Exactly! It was what made it so great.

Chance pointed to the samples of his proposed maple cabinets and black granite countertops, the top-of-the-line stainless steel appliances and plentiful pantry shelving. "It'll get the job done, Mom."

Where he had been trying to be economical, his competition had gone all out. Dual dishwashers, two prep areas, double ovens and countless other features. Everywhere you looked there was some sort of up-charge.

Lucille smiled. "Molly captured what I was looking for. Unfortunately, I don't think she and her crew can manage to finish the entire downstairs in the next five weeks."

Molly's triumph faded. "Did you say five... weeks?"

Lucille nodded. "I want to reserve December

19 for delivery of the furniture from my previous house in Dallas that's currently in storage, the twentieth and the twenty-first for decorating and the twenty-second for my planned fundraiser for the Lockhart Foundation and West Texas Warrior Assistance program. And of course Christmas Eve and Day for my family celebration."

Chance frowned. "Which means all the wiring, plumbing, drywall and paint, as well as kitchen and master suite bath, will have to go in by then."

His mother remained undaunted. "You have six people on your crew, Chance. Molly has seven. If you have all thirteen people working, it's easily feasible. I'll pay overtime if necessary."

All business, Molly nodded. "How are we going to divide the work?"

Matter-of-factly, Lucille explained, "Molly will be in charge of the design and the materials, and Chance will supervise the construction and installation. Then, of course, Molly, I'd like you to do the yuletide decorating." She flashed a smile her way. "I'll give you a free hand with that since part of the reason for the rush is to help you showcase your skills during the fundraising open house, and make the connections with my Dallas friends that will help you drum up business there."

Chance turned to his mother and gave her a warning look. He would have expected Lucille, who, better than anyone, knew the downside of leaving the warm, supportive utopia of Laramie County behind, to be urging caution. Not cheerleading. "You're really supporting Molly in this lunacy?" he blurted before he could stop himself.

Molly had a growing business. A home. Dozens of people who looked out for her. A young son who was thriving in the small-town environment. Why she would want to leave all that for the coldness of the big city he had grown up in was beyond him.

"I wouldn't call it that." Lucille regarded him sternly. "And, yes, I fully understand Molly's desire to be all that she can be."

Resolved to inject a little common sense into the conversation, Chance scoffed, "In terms of what? Money? Social position?"

Molly glared at him. "Don't forget dazzling professional success! And all the accoutrements that come with it."

Chance looked heavenward. "I don't expect you to understand," Molly said stiffly, her emotions suddenly as fired up as his.

"Good," Chance snapped back, running his hand through his hair in exasperation. Then, pinning her with a glare of his own, he said exactly what was on his mind. "Because I don't."

Chapter Two

"Avoiding me?" a husky voice taunted.

Molly thought work had wrapped up for the day. Which was, as it turned out, the only reason she was at the Circle H ranch house this late.

Turning in the direction of the familiar baritone, Molly took in the sight of the indomitable cowboy. Clad in a knit thermal tee, plaid flannel shirt and jeans, a tool belt circling his waist, Chance Lockhart strode toward her purposefully.

Working to still her racing heart, Molly held

her clipboard and pen close to her chest. She lifted her chin. "Why would you think that?"

Chance stopped just short of her and gave her a slow, thorough once-over. "We've both had crews working here ten days straight, and you and I haven't run into each other once."

Thank God.

Aware the last thing she wanted was to give Chance another opportunity to tell her what he thought of her plan to improve her and her son's lives, Molly shrugged. "I guess we have different schedules."

His, she had deduced, kept him at his ranch, taking care of his bucking bulls early mornings and evenings. Hence, it was usually safe to arrive at the remodeling site during those hours.

Except today, he'd varied his routine. Why? To try to catch her in person, rather than communicate through endless emails and texts?

What she knew for certain was that it would be dark in another fifteen minutes, and all she had for light was a 220-volt camping lantern.

As seemingly unaffected by their quiet, intimate surroundings as the cell phone that kept going off with a sound that usually signaled an incoming text message—checked, then unanswered—in the holster at his waist, he glanced around. "What do you think thus far?"

That even with rumpled hair and a couple of days' growth of beard on your face, you are without a doubt the sexiest man I've ever seen. Which was too bad. Molly sighed inwardly, since Chance wasn't at all her type. But if he were…she could definitely lose herself in those gorgeous hazel eyes, big hunky body and wickedly sensual lips. Luckily he didn't know that.

With effort, she switched on her camping lantern, set it on the floor and got out her tape measure. She measured the front windows and door for window treatments and wreaths. The fireplace and staircase for garlands. Jotting down the numbers in her leather notebook, she said, "I think our combined crews have made amazing progress."

Under Chance's direction, new rooms had been framed out and a first-floor powder room for guests added last minute. Plumbing and electrical wiring had been installed, new drywall put up and taped, crown molding and trim work done.

Chance moved to the fireplace. He ran his big, calloused hand along the new wooden mantel. It was cut out of the same rustic oak as the support beams overhead. "The floors will be repaired where needed and sanded tomorrow."

Which took them all the way up to Thanksgiving, she knew. The one day every one of them would have a break from the demanding schedule.

"You got the tile for the kitchen and the bathrooms, and the paint colors picked out?"

Trying not to think what he would be doing for the holidays, Molly replied, "Still waiting on final approval from your mom. She wants to see samples in the light here before she decides. But we've narrowed it down to a couple of shades for each space."

Chance ambled over and switched on several of the portable construction lamps. "The new appliances and light fixtures?"

Instantly the downstairs became much brighter. "On order."

He walked around, inspecting some of the work that had been done. Finding a tiny flaw, he stuck a piece of blue painter's tape on it. "Kitchen and bath cabinets and countertops?"

"Will all be delivered in time to meet our schedule."

He nodded, as aware as she that one major glitch could throw everything off. Fortunately, thus far anyway, luck had been completely on their side.

He came toward her.

Her heartbeat picked up for no reason she could figure. Molly cleared her throat. "Speaking of the holiday... I wanted to talk to you about Thanksgiving." She moved around restlessly. "I've given my crew the day off."

Joining her at the hearth, Chance took a foil-wrapped candy from his shirt pocket. "Same here."

There was no way, she thought, he could know that was her very favorite. Trying not to salivate over the treat, Molly continued, "But they've all agreed to work on Friday."

He nodded, ripping open one end. Immediately the smell of dark chocolate and peppermint filled the small space between them.

"Mine, too."

Chance's cell phone buzzed again, this time with the ringtone "I Saw Mommy Kissing Santa Claus."

Telling herself that particular choice in no way involved her, either, Molly watched as, once again, he checked the screen and ignored it.

He held out the partially unwrapped confection. "Want one?" he asked.

Now she knew he was flirting.

"I've got another..." he teased.

Hell, yes, she wanted some of his dark chocolate peppermint. But if she started taking candy from him on a whim, who knew what might be next?

She returned his assessing look and said as innocently as possible, "Thanks, but no."

His eyes gleamed.

"I don't really like those."

His sexy grin widened all the more.

Then his phone buzzed yet again. With the maddeningly suggestive holiday song...

Thinking maybe he really should answer that, and would if she weren't standing right there, Molly picked up her lantern before she ended up doing something really stupid—like kissing the smug look off his face—and headed for the staircase.

Able to feel the heat of his masculine gaze drifting over her, she tossed the words over her shoulder. "I've got to measure the upstairs windows before I go."

"Want help?"

"No!"

He chuckled, as she had known he would.

Molly fought back a flush. This was exactly why she had been avoiding him. Luckily she had work to keep her busy. Chance might even be gone before she left.

She had just finished measuring the first window when she heard a door open, then close. Lucille Lockhart's lyrical voice echoed through the first floor. "Chance? Why aren't you picking up? I just got another call from Babs Holcombe. She said she's been trying to reach you for days!"

Who the heck is Babs? Not that she should be listening...

"Been a little busy, Mom," Chance growled.

Lucille's high heels tapped across the wood floors. "You owe her the courtesy of a return call. Or at the very least an email!"

"After the way things ended with Delia?" Chance scoffed.

Delia? Molly perked up, edging a little closer despite herself.

"I admit that wasn't one of their finer moments," Lucille conceded reluctantly, "but they've both done a lot to support the Lockhart Foundation in the three years since."

"Okay," Chance countered gruffly.

"Okay you'll call her," Lucille pressed, sounding beside herself with irritation, "or okay you won't?"

Silence reigned once again.

Molly could imagine the bullheaded look on Chance's face. The disapproving moue of his mother. There was a brief murmur of disgruntled talk she couldn't decipher, then the sound of Lucille leaving. The front door shut. Chance's heavy footsteps crossed to the center of the house. "You can come down now!" he called cheerfully up the stairs.

Aghast that he knew she had been eavesdropping, heat flooded her cheeks. Measurements taken, she walked back down, pocketing her pen. "Sorry. Didn't mean to intrude."

He gave her a look that said, "I'll bet."

Falling into step beside her, he accompanied her out onto the front porch. The air had the distinct damp chill of late November. Dark clouds gathered along the horizon, where the sun was setting in streaks of purple and gray.

"How is Braden doing? Were you able to steer him toward the Leo and Lizzie World Adventure train set?"

Surprised that Chance recalled the name of the toy, Molly grimaced. "Ah, no. Not yet."

Concern etched his ruggedly handsome face. "Meaning you haven't really tried yet?"

Molly only wished that were the case. Taking her first real break of the day, she perched on the railing edging the front porch. "Meaning, like with most men, subtlety doesn't work on Braden. Nor does direct conversation."

Chance took a seat opposite her, mesmerizing her with the blatant interest in his eyes. "So he still wants a live baby bull and a momma."

"As well as a daddy bull."

"Wow."

She sighed, relieved to be able to talk about what had been bothering her all day. "Wow is right."

His expression grew thoughtful. "What are you going to do?"

With effort, she forced herself to meet his probing gaze. "Honestly? I don't have a clue."

"I had a few ideas."

Molly pushed to her feet. Feeling her pulse skitter, she turned her head to the side. "I think you've done enough," she quipped, using sarcasm to hide her worry.

He accompanied her down the steps to her SUV. "Seriously. I think I might be able to dissuade him, given another opportunity. And since you have Thanksgiving Day off and so do I, and my mother is hosting her annual dinner at the bunkhouse, I was thinking you and Braden might want to come as my plus two."

Aware the mood between them was quickly becoming highly charged and way too intimate, Molly unlocked her vehicle. "You're asking me for a date?"

To her consternation, he didn't exactly deny it.

"There will be a lot of people there. Three of my siblings and their significant others and or friends. And a few other family friends."

Molly tossed her bag into the front passenger seat. "First of all, your mother and I get along so well because I know my place."

His brow lifted.

"Furthermore, Braden and I have our own holiday tradition."

He rested a muscular forearm on the open driver-side door. "You cook?"

Molly lifted her chin. "I take him to the buffet at the cafeteria in San Angelo."

Sympathy lit his gaze. "Sounds…lonely."

Lonely, Molly thought, was being a fifth wheel

at the big family gatherings of friends. Knowing, you'd never enjoy the same.

She shrugged. "Crowded is more like it. But it's not too bad if we get there at eleven, when it opens, and then Braden and I have the rest of the day to do whatever we want." Which usually involved a family activity of their own.

Chance stepped back. "Well, if you change your mind, the invitation stands."

Molly slid behind the wheel. "Thanks, but I won't." She looked up at him.

Whether Chance admitted it or not, she was out of his league socially, too. "And don't worry about Braden. I'll figure out a way to handle his misconceptions about what is possible for Christmas. And what is not."

EXCEPT SHE WASN'T handling it, Molly thought the following day when they entered the popular San Angelo cafeteria. At least not as well as she or her son would like.

"I'm hungry, Mommy," Braden complained as the line of customers inched forward.

Although she had been hoping to make this Thanksgiving really special for him, he'd been grumpy since waking that morning. "I know." Molly inched up slightly, clear of the entrance. "It will be our turn soon. See?" She pointed to the lighted display cases up ahead.

Braden stamped his cowboy boot. "Don't want to wait," he fumed.

"I know." Thinking he might be overheated, Molly knelt down in front of him and unzipped his fleece hoodie. She figured he would be fine once they sat down. Avoiding a meltdown before that concerned her.

"Can we go home now?" Braden persisted.

"Oh, you don't want to do that," a familiar low voice said from behind them. "I hear the holiday buffet here is not to be missed."

Braden lit up like a Christmas tree. "Cowboy Chance!"

"Hi, buddy!" Chance held out his palm. Braden high-fived him.

Slowly, Molly straightened to her full height. To her dismay, she was ridiculously glad to see him. Especially looking so fine.

Like her, he had upped his game a notch. Slacks, a starched shirt, tie and tweed Western-cut blazer, instead of his usual flannel shirt and jeans. "Aren't you supposed to be at your mom's today?"

"Already made my appearance."

Which accounted for his neatly combed chestnut hair and freshly shaven jaw.

"I'm tired," Braden complained.

Molly inhaled the sandalwood and leather fragrance of Chance's cologne, mixing with the usual soap and fresh air scent of his skin.

"Probably a little bored, too." Chance winked. He reached into his jacket pockets. "Which is why I brought you these." He pulled out a toy reindeer with a big red nose and a coordinating winter sleigh.

Braden beamed. "Rudolph!"

Molly gave Chance a look her delighted son could not see. "What are you doing?" she demanded sweetly.

Grooves deepened on either side of his mouth. "Working on that solution."

Aware how easy it would be to fall for this sexy cowboy's charms, Molly stiffened. "I fail to see how—"

He clapped a hand on her shoulder. "All in good time, my darlin'. All in good time. And—" he nodded at the space behind her "—you're going to want to move on up."

The line was indeed pushing forward.

Molly inched ahead. "I don't remember inviting you," she murmured so only he could hear, while her son energetically played with the reindeer and sleigh.

Chance leaned down to whisper in her ear. "That's the good thing about having Thanksgiving here. You don't need an invite." He looked around, impressed. "Although given how crowded the establishment is quickly getting, it would probably be considerate of the three of us to share a table, rather than unnecessarily take up more chairs than we need."

"You're impossible." Despite herself, she was glad to see him.

Braden tugged on Chance's blazer. He tilted his head back so he could see his idol's face. "Thank you for toys."

Chance ruffled her son's hair. "You're welcome, buddy. It was my pleasure."

To Molly's surprise, it was hers, too.

"So what next?" Chance asked as the three of them finished their turkey dinners.

Molly looked out the cafeteria windows. The rain that had been threatening since the previous evening had started midmeal. It was now coming down in sheets. She sighed. "No playground, unfortunately..."

Braden stopped playing with the toys Chance

had brought him long enough to scowl. "Promised!"

Molly used a napkin to wipe some cranberry sauce off her son's chin. "I know, honey, but everything will be all wet, so we'll have to do something indoors."

"Bouncy house?"

"Afraid not. It's closed because today is a holiday."

"Cowboy Chance play. My house."

She did have activities planned there, two they had already started, in fact, in addition to Braden's usual time set aside to do whatever he wanted. "I'm sure Mr. Chance has other things to do, honey."

He met her eyes. "Not really." Chance turned back to Braden, his cordial tone as reassuring as his presence. "What kind of toys do you have?"

"Trucks and cars."

"Trains?"

Braden shook his head.

Abruptly Molly saw where Chance was going with this.

If he did have an idea how to convince her son to yearn for the holiday gift she had chosen for Braden...could she afford to turn Chance down? Especially if the end result was Braden's happiness?

Braden tugged on her sleeve. "Go now, Mommy!" He stood on his chair and held out his arms to their lunch companion. "Cowboy Chance, too!"

Chance caught Braden in his big arms.

Trying not to think how natural the two looked together, Molly said, "We won't expect you to stay long."

Chance stood, Braden still in his arms. "I won't wear out my welcome. On the other hand..." He winked and shrugged in a way that opened up a ton of possibilities. A shiver of awareness swept through her. He probably would be a good time, Molly thought despite herself. Too good a time.

She shook off the awareness. Stacking their

dishes and trays, she asked, "You know where I live?"

He nodded, looking as unexpectedly content in that moment as she felt. "Spring Street in Laramie."

MOLLY LED THE WAY. The drive back to Laramie took thirty-five minutes. It was still raining when Chance parked behind Molly's SUV and got out of his pickup truck.

Her home, a former carriage house, sported a three-foot-high white picket fence and was sandwiched between two large Victorians. The one-story abode, while much smaller and set back a ways from the sidewalk, was just as attractive—if not more so—than every other home on the prestigious street. A front porch with white wicker furniture spanned the width of the thousand-square-foot house, which featured gray clapboard sides, white trim and black shutters.

The scent of fresh-cut pine hit Chance the moment he walked in the door.

A Christmas tree stood in the corner of the comfortably outfitted living area, boxes of lights and decorations beside it.

The state-of-the-art kitchen, situated at the back of the main living area, was banked by a wall of floor-to-ceiling windows that flooded the small, cozy space with light. Plentiful cabinets, painted a dark slate, and an island that also served as a dining area were a nice counterpoint to the white quartz countertops, bleached wood floors and stainless steel appliances.

Standing there, noting how beautiful her home was, he couldn't imagine why she would ever want to leave it.

Her son, however, had other things on his mind.

Barely standing still long enough for his mother to wrestle him out of his damp rain jacket, he set his Rudolph and sleigh on the coffee table, next to a soft blue blanket, then headed importantly for the kitchen, where a delicious fresh dough and orange smell emanated. "Come on, Mr. Chance. We cook!"

Braden grabbed a tyke-size navy chef's apron off the hook, and then handed Chance one, as well—frilly and floral. "Put on!" he demanded.

Molly's amused expression dared Chance to do so.

Clearly, he noted, she did not think he would. Which just showed how much she knew. "Sure thing, buddy," Chance agreed drily, pulling the garment over his head. The cloth barely covered his broad chest, and the waist hit him at mid-sternum. Tying it seemed impossible, given the fact he couldn't find the strings.

Grinning, Molly stepped behind him. "Allow me."

Her hands brushed his spine as she secured it in place. His body reacted as if they'd kissed. Fortunately, she was too on task to notice. She opened a drawer and pulled out a plain white chef's apron, that was, as it happened, much more his size.

She tilted her head, her gaze moving over him humorously. "Want to trade?"

Aware this was the first time he'd seen her eyes sparkle so mischievously, he motioned for her to turn so he could tie her apron strings, too. She needed to goof around like this more often. Not be so serious all the time. "Nah, I'm good."

The three of them took turns washing their hands; then Braden climbed onto the step stool next to the island. "Ready, Mommy?" the tyke asked eagerly.

"Let's see." Molly pulled a linen towel away from the top of a large bowl. Inside was a billowy cloud of dough. "I think so."

She positioned the bowl in front of her son. "Ready to punch it down?"

With a gleeful shout, Braden went to town, pummeling the buttery dough until all the air was released. "What are we making?" Chance asked. It sure smelled good, even at this early stage.

Molly moved close enough he could catch a

whiff of her perfume. It was every bit as feminine and enticing and delectable as she was.

"Christmas *stollen*." She tilted her head curiously. "Ever had it?"

"I don't think so."

"Well, you're in for a treat." She turned the dough onto a floured wooden board and divided it into three sections—which she quickly rolled out into long loaves. Wordlessly, she retrieved a bowl of dried cherries, cranberries and almonds, soaking in what appeared to be orange juice, and drained the excess. "Time to sprinkle on the extras."

Braden—no novice at baking—positioned his fruit and nuts very seriously, dropping them one by one onto the dough. "You, too, Cowboy Chance."

"Yes, sir," Chance said, soberly following Braden's lead. Molly joined in.

When they'd finished, Braden clapped his hands. "I done now, Mommy?"

"Yes. You did a very good job." She wiped

his hands with a clean cloth. "You can go play while I get this ready for the second rise."

He hurried off to retrieve his Rudolph and sleigh. Then he brought out his toy dump truck to give them a ride.

With Braden playing happily, Chance settled on a stool at the island. "Where did you learn to do this?"

"My mother taught me." Molly showed him how to knead the dough until it was soft and elastic, and then shape it into loaves. Carefully, he followed her lead. "Her grandparents emigrated here from Germany. Baking was an important part of their holiday tradition, and she passed it on to me, as her mother had to her."

Remembering his earlier faux pas, he trod carefully. "Where is your mom now?"

Sorrow pinched Molly's face. "She died of meningitis when I was fourteen. My dad never really got over the loss, and he died in a car accident just before I graduated from high school."

He wished he had been around to comfort her, but that had been years before he'd moved to Laramie. "That must have been rough."

"It was." Molly carefully transferred the loaves onto baking sheets and covered them with linen cloths, the actions of her hands delicate and sure. "But I had a lot of help from the people in the community. The local bank gave me a second mortgage on this house, so I'd have somewhere to live, and enough funds to get by on while I studied construction and interior design at the local community college and did what was necessary to obtain my general contractor's license."

His gaze drifted over her. She wore a long-sleeved emerald dress that made the most of her stunning curves, black tights and flats. Her auburn hair was curlier than usual—he supposed it was the rain. "What made you want to pursue that?"

Molly lounged against the counter, her hands braced on either side of her. "Tradition, I guess.

My mom taught classes in nutrition and cooking at Laramie High, and she did interior design work on the side, and my dad was a general contractor who did mostly handyman work."

She paused to rub a spot of flour from her hip. "Following in their footsteps made me feel closer to them. Plus, both my parents had substantial client lists that I initially utilized to get work. So I was able to get on my feet financially a lot faster than I would have otherwise."

Braden walked into the kitchen. He stepped between them merrily. "Puddles, Mommy?"

Grinning, Molly looked out the window. The rain that had been landing in torrents was now coming down gently. "You want to go outside?"

Braden nodded.

"Then let's get you suited up." Molly walked into the mudroom off the garage, then returned with a pair of yellow rain boots, matching slicker and wide-brimmed hat. Braden brimmed with anticipation. "You come, too, Cowboy Chance?"

"We'll both watch you from the front porch," Molly promised. "Unless…" She paused to look at Chance. "You have somewhere else you need to be?"

Chapter Three

This was Chance's opportunity to make a graceful exit.

To his surprise, he wasn't in a hurry to leave. In fact, he was sort of lamenting the fact that the time would eventually come. "Actually," Chance admitted good-naturedly, "I was hoping I'd be able to see what the Christmas *stollen* looks like when it's finished."

"Yummy!" Braden declared, rubbing his tummy.

Chance chuckled. The little buckaroo's enthusiasm was infectious. "You think so?"

Braden nodded magnanimously. "We share. Mommy. Me. You."

Chance turned to Molly. "Is that okay?" he asked casually, wanting to give her the option of throwing him out—if that was what she wanted.

"You probably should see what you've been missing," she said drily.

He had an inkling. And he wasn't just thinking about baked goods.

"Outside?" Braden asked again, impatiently.

"Let's go." She grabbed a rain jacket for herself, then opened the door. A blast of unexpectedly warm air hit them. No doubt brought in by the front. "I was going to offer you a cup of coffee," Molly said, looping the jacket over a wicker chair, "but maybe it should be iced tea."

"Coffee's fine." Chance smiled. "Thanks."

Molly watched her son march down the front steps and out into the light rain. They both grinned as Braden lifted his face to the sky and stuck out his tongue to catch a few raindrops. Fondly, Molly shook her head, then turned back to Chance. "Can you keep an eye on Braden for a minute? He knows not to go outside of the picket fence."

"No problem." Chance took the seat she indicated on the front porch. For the next few minutes, he watched Braden investigate everything from the water running out of the gutters to the drops pearling on the leafy green shrubs.

He'd forgotten what it felt like to look at the world with such unvarnished appreciation.

Maybe it was time he remembered...

"Sure you wouldn't rather be at your mom's watching football with your brothers?" Molly teased, returning with a tray containing a carafe, two mugs, sugar and cream. She set it on the table between them.

Chance grinned at her son, who was now hopscotching his way through a series of puddles on the front walk.

He turned his attention back to Molly. Her

cheeks flushed with happiness, her auburn hair slightly mussed, a smudge of flour across one cheek, she had never looked more beautiful. Or content.

He liked seeing her this way.

"Oh, there's no football at my mom's on Thanksgiving."

Her delicate brow pleated. "Seriously?"

As she neared, he caught the fragrance of her lavender hand soap mingling with the sweet, sexy scent of her hair and skin. Pushing the electric awareness away, Chance sat back in his chair. "She says that's why DVRs were invented. Social events require socializing properly with each other, not tuning everyone out watching TV."

Molly handed him a mug of steaming coffee. She wrinkled her nose at him. "Sounds like Lucille."

Chance watched as she settled in the chair beside his. The hem of her knit dress rode up a little. She crossed her legs at the knee and tugged it down discreetly, but not before he had seen enough of her long slender thighs to make his heart race.

Chance worked to keep his mind on the conversation. "No doubt about it. My mother's big on etiquette, always has been."

Molly waved at her son, who was now marching around the perimeter of the inside of the fence. Braden stopped to lift his arms high and turn his face to the slowly clearing sky overhead. "Still, the menu would probably have been better..."

Chance couldn't recall when he had enjoyed a holiday meal more. "I thought we had a fine meal at the cafeteria. Turkey. All the trimmings. Not to mention choice of dessert."

She chuckled, holding her mug against the softness of her full lips. "You did have two pieces of pie."

He watched her blow lightly on her coffee, then take a dainty sip. Shrugged. "Couldn't make up my mind."

He was certain about one thing, though.

He wanted to ravish Molly Griffith.

And would…

"Look, Mommy!" Braden shouted. "Rainbow!"

They both turned in the direction he was pointing. Sure enough, there was one arcing across the sky.

"Come here, Mommy! Come see!"

"Just when I wish I had my camera out," she murmured with a rueful grin, rising to join her son.

Not wanting to intrude, Chance stayed behind to make her wish come true.

CHANCE LOCKHART WAS full of surprises, Molly thought minutes later, looking at the series of action photos he had taken on his cell phone while she and Braden had admired the burst of colors streaking across the late afternoon sky.

"Thank you for capturing that moment," Molly said softly when they walked back inside a few minutes later to put the *stollen* in the oven. Chance had not only gotten several nice shots of her and Braden together—something that rarely happened on the spur of the moment since she had no other family member to do the honor—but he'd also managed to capture a close-up of the wonder on her little boy's face.

Priceless.

"I thought you would want to remember it. Not every day you see a rainbow on Thanksgiving."

Not every day she spent a holiday with such a sweet, handsome man. Not that this was a date. Even if it had started to feel like a date.

Molly finished getting Braden out of his rain gear, then showed her little boy the photos Chance had taken on his phone and emailed to her.

"That's me," Braden said gleefully. "And Mommy!" He pushed the phone away. "Can we dec'rate tree?"

That had been her original plan.

Chance shrugged his broad shoulders affably. "I'm up for it if you are," he said.

"You're really into Christmas, aren't you?" She hadn't met many single guys who were.

Or were this kind to her son.

"Hey." Chance aimed a thumb at the center of his chest. "When the opportunity to be chivalrous presents itself..."

He was on board, Molly thought. Which just went to show how badly she had misjudged the gorgeous cowboy.

By the time the oven timer went off half an hour later, they had the lights strung and on. Half a dozen ornaments later, the fruit-and-nut-studded pastry was cool enough to finish.

Aprons went back on. Although this time Molly made sure that Chance had the larger garment. Together, they all brushed on melted butter, then sprinkled the tops of their masterpieces with granulated sugar.

"And now for the pièce de résistance!" Molly declared triumphantly, showing her son how to use the sifter to cover the pastry with a final snowy-white cover of confectioner's sugar. She handed the sifter to Chance, watched as he did the same to his and then followed suit.

The three pastries made a lovely, Christmassy sight.

"Eat now?" Braden asked.

Molly grinned. "Let's taste it." She cut off a two-inch slice for Braden, a larger one for Chance and a slightly smaller one for herself.

They all bit down on the soft, citrus-flavored nut-and-fruit bread with the sweet and slightly crunchy exterior. "Wow." Chance's hazel eyes lit up. "That's…amazing."

"Yummy," Braden agreed.

Molly had to admit, between the three of them they had done a good job. Before she could think, she offered, "Want to take a loaf home with you?"

Luckily he didn't read any extra meaning into her impulsive gesture. An affable grin deepened the crinkles around his eyes. "Sure you don't mind?"

Remembering what her late mother had told her—that the way to a man's heart was through his stomach—Molly shrugged off the importance. "I'll be baking all month long."

His gaze skimmed her appreciatively. "In that case—" he winked "—I'll have to remember to come around more often."

Molly caught her breath at the implication.

Was he truly interested in her?

She knew she desired him. Always had. Even though they were clearly all wrong for each other. Still…

"All done, Mommy!"

Switching quickly back to parenting mode, Molly gently wiped the sugar from her son's hands and face. Braden reclaimed the Rudolph and sleigh, along with his favorite blue blankie. Yawning, he snuggled on the sofa.

Chance arched an inquisitive brow. "Nap time?"

"Two hours ago," Molly confirmed softly, watching Braden struggle to keep his eyes open.

"Oh." A wealth of emotion—and understanding—in a single word.

"Yeah. I was hoping—" Molly moved closer to Chance, whispering even more quietly "—he'd be able to get through the day without one. Especially since it's so late."

Chance shook his head fondly. Putting an easy hand on Molly's shoulder, he nodded in the direction of the couch. "Looks like he's already asleep."

Molly took in the sight of her child, blissfully cuddled up, auburn lashes fanning across his cheek. She sighed. "Indeed, he is."

Chance caressed her shoulder lightly. "That's a problem?"

Molly's heart raced at the casual contact. "He'll be grouchy when I do wake him up before dinner and may have trouble falling asleep tonight."

"Anything I can do?"

If you were here, sure. You won't be. Molly looked up at Chance. Time seemed to suspend. Suddenly there was just the two of them. "Cross your fingers for me?"

His eyes darkened. He brushed his thumb across her lower lip and continued to regard her steadily. "How about something even better?" he said huskily, lifting her hand to his lips. He pressed a kiss across her knuckles. She caught her breath. And then she was in his arms. Wrapping both his hands around her small waist, he caught her against him, so they were length to length.

Molly's breath hitched again.

"Chance," she whispered.

His head lowered. Slowly. Purposefully. "Just one, darlin'..." He tunneled his hands through her hair and his eyes shuttered. "That's all I'm asking."

Molly saw the kiss coming, and she knew she should do something to stop it. She was attracted to Chance enough already. If his lips were to actually touch hers…

With a small, sharp intake of breath, she lifted both hands and spread them across the muscular warmth of his broad chest. His heart was beating, strong and steady. His head lowered even more. And then there was no stopping it. Their lips connected, and a shiver of pure delight went through her. Her usual caution gone, she opened her mouth to the seductive pressure of his. He tasted like rich black coffee and freshly baked *stollen*. And man. And she could no more deny him than she could deny herself. It was Thanksgiving, after all. A day to count blessings. Be happy. Thankful. At ease. And she'd never felt more at ease than she did at that very moment.

Chance knew he was taking advantage, that Molly deserved a lot better than the overture he was making. He also knew opportunities like this did not come along all that often.

Molly had a wall around her heart, strong enough to keep the entire male species at bay.

She was driven by fierce ambition. And a robust little chaperone that kept her on the straight and narrow.

Had he spent time with her before now, he would have realized what a beautiful, complicated and magnificent woman she was.

He would have known there was a lot more to her than her need for tremendous financial security, and the social status that came with it. But he hadn't, so he had squandered the two years he had resided in Laramie County. Two years in which he could have pursued her like she was meant to be pursued.

Fortunately, he still had a month left.

He wasn't going to waste it.

Or make any more mistakes.

So he kissed her passionately until she kissed him back and curled against him. And it was only then, when they started to make the kind of connection that rocked both their worlds, that she suddenly gasped and wrenched her lips from his.

"Is this the point where you haul off and slap me across the face?" Chance joked.

It was definitely the point where she gave herself a good hard shake, Molly thought. What in all Texas had gotten into her? She couldn't start getting involved with someone! Or even have a fling. Not when she was getting ready to leave rural Laramie County and build a life in the city.

Reluctantly, she stepped out of the warm cocoon of Chance's strong arms. She went to a drawer on the opposite side of the kitchen and pulled out a roll of plastic wrap.

Her lips and body still throbbing from the thrilling contact, she lifted a staying hand and admitted softly, "That was my fault every bit as much as it was yours."

"Fault?" With displeasure, he zeroed in on her low, censoring tone.

"Holidays can be really lonely."

He gave her a considering look. "They don't have to be."

Irritated he saw so much of her feelings when

she wanted him to see so little, Molly admitted, "It's easy to find yourself reaching out in ways you normally wouldn't."

His eyes filled with a mixture of curiosity and compassion. "Is that what happened with Braden's daddy?"

"No," Molly said, trying hard not to succumb to the unexpected tenderness in Chance's expression.

He leaned against the counter, arms folded in front of him, and continued to study her. "Then?"

Maybe if Chance knew the worst about her, he would forget the sizzling physical attraction between them and realize their backgrounds were too diverse for them to ever be more than casual friends.

Molly drew a deep breath. "I don't want to go down the wrong path again."

"With me."

It upset her to bring this up, but she knew for both their sakes, it had to be said. Chance had to start facing the fact they were and always would be all wrong for each other. "With anyone who was born outside my social standing."

His brow furrowed. "You really think I'm that much of a snob?"

She flushed and dropped her gaze to his muscular chest. "I think, in this respect, you might be as naive as I once was."

"I'm listening," he said.

Molly grabbed the spray cleaner and paper towels, then began scrubbing down the counters. "I never really dated much after my dad died. I was too busy trying to put myself through school and get my business going."

He moved so she could reach behind him. But not quite enough. As she reached, her shoulder lightly brushed his bicep. "Sounds like you had to grow up pretty fast."

Molly straightened. "All that changed when Aaron Powell III came to Laramie to look for lakeside property that could be flipped." She grimaced at the memory. "I was asked to give a bid. I did and won the work on several houses that he and his family purchased." She removed her apron and hung it back on the hook. Recalling her first taste of unfettered luxury, she admitted reluctantly, "I'd never been friends with anyone that ostentatiously wealthy, and Aaron swept me off my feet."

Chance's expression relaxed in understanding. "How long were you together?"

"About three months."

Taking her by the hand, he guided her onto the stool. Sat down beside her. "You didn't expect it to end?"

Molly shrugged, still wishing she hadn't been quite so naive. Shifting so the two of them faced each other, she said, "I knew Aaron's life was in Houston, that his shuttling back and forth continuously would stop when my work was done and the lake properties were listed. But I was okay with that. I was perfectly willing to move where he was."

Chance's expression darkened. "He didn't want that."

Humiliation clogged Molly's throat. "He didn't think that would go over so well with his fiancée."

An awkward silence fell.

"You had no idea," Chance guessed in a low, even tone.

"None," Molly was forced to admit. Restless, she got up and began to pace the confines of the kitchen. "Unfortunately, I was pregnant by then. And I'd already told him."

Giving Chance no more opportunity to ask questions, Molly rushed on. "The next thing I know the Powell family lawyer is at my door with a contract for me to sign. All I have to do is agree—in writing—not to ever publicly acknowledge paternity and a nice six-figure check is mine."

Jaw taut, Chance stood. "I'm pretty sure that's not legal."

Molly nodded as he circled the counter and strode closer.

"I could have forced the issue in court. I also knew if I did that, Aaron and his attorneys would use my modest financial circumstances to allege I was a gold digger and make our lives a living hell. My only priority was to protect my child from hurt."

The compassion in Chance's hazel eyes spurred her to go on.

"So I hired a lawyer and countered with an offer of my own. I would never pursue any claims of paternity, or child support, if Aaron would promise to do the same and allow me to raise Braden completely on my own." She drew a breath. "Aaron was more than happy with that, since he didn't really want children, never mind a bastard son from a woman from a lower social echelon." Molly wrung her hands and lifted her chin defiantly. "So we signed an agreement... and that was that."

Chance searched her face. "Did you ever regret it?"

Wasn't that the million-dollar question!

Molly shrugged, the barriers coming up to protect her heart once again. Steadily, she held Chance's gaze. "I regret mistaking big, expensive romantic gestures for love. And the fact that Braden doesn't have the devoted daddy he deserves."

His gaze drifted over her, igniting wildfires wherever it landed. "The latter could be fixed," he pointed out matter-of-factly.

Maybe someday. For the first time, she was beginning to see that.

In the meantime, she had the next phase of her life plan to execute. Molly handed Chance the wrapped, freshly baked *stollen* and escorted him to the door. Wary of her still-sleeping son, she eased it open, then stepped with him all the way out onto the porch. It was unseasonably warm, and the sun sparkled down on them.

"The point is, even if fate works against us

and Braden never gets the loving daddy he deserves, I still have to support my son to the very
best of my ability."

"Which means?" Chance prodded, suddenly
looking a lot less pleased.

Molly said determinedly, "I've got to move to
a place where I can make a lot more money than
I am now. And give Braden the kind of boundless future that he deserves."

And that meant no more getting too friendly
with Chance.

And definitely no more kissing him!

Chapter Four

"How was your Thanksgiving?" Chance asked the two newest members of the Bullhaven family, now temporarily quartered in a private pasture at the Circle H.

"Mine was the best I've ever had." He set out premium feed. "You think I'm exaggerating, but I'm not."

Even though Molly had sort of kicked him out at the end, he'd left with a warm feeling in his chest that had continued through the night and had still lingered there when he woke up, maybe because he was going to see her again soon.

"Yeah, yeah, you're right. I've got it bad…" But there were worse things than knowing what you wanted. And what he wanted right now was a Christmas holiday spent with Molly. And her adorable son.

The momma Black Angus came toward the bucket, her bull calf, Mistletoe Jr., at her side. While she ate, the calf searched for a teat. Momma mooed gently in approval and then licked at her calf as it started to nurse.

Satisfied all was well, Chance went to his pickup truck. The morning was slightly cool, and rain had left the air smelling clean and brisk. He got out the rest of his breakfast—a thick wedge of Christmas bread—and a thermos of hot black coffee.

Leaning against the fender, he enjoyed the early morning quiet. Until his brother Wyatt drove up and parked beside him. An ornery look on his face, he nodded at the confection in Chance's hand. "What's that?"

Chance savored another bite. *"Stollen."*

Wyatt blinked. "A—what?"

Chance let the citrus-flavored bread melt on his tongue. "It's a German Christmas bread made with fruit and nuts."

Wyatt nodded, practically salivating now. "Looks good," he said.

It was more than simply good, Chance thought. It was the most amazing thing he had ever eaten. Better yet was the fact he had helped Molly and Braden make it.

"Can I have some?" Ready to help himself, Wyatt ambled closer.

Chance held it out of reach. "Sorry."

Wyatt blinked in surprise. It wasn't like his brother to be greedy. "What do you mean no?" he demanded.

Chance moved farther away. "I'm not sharing."

His brother stared at him as if he'd grown two heads. "Why the devil not?"

Chance shrugged as Molly's car turned into

the lane and parked in front of the Circle H ranch house, too. "Just not."

She emerged from the driver's side, looking as stunning as usual in a pair of faded jeans, a long-sleeved white T-shirt and a cropped denim jacket. She had a pair of fancy burgundy engineer boots on, a tape measure attached to her belt and a pen stuck behind one ear. Clearly she was ready to work.

Wyatt angled a thumb at him as she approached. "Can you believe this?" Wyatt grumbled. "Chance is eating *stollen* and refusing to share."

Mischief lit her pretty amber eyes when her gaze fell to the treat in his hand. Chance gave her a look, imploring her not to give his brother information to dissect. What he and Molly had experienced was too special, too fragile, to risk or share.

The corners of her lips turning up all the more, she sipped coffee from the travel mug in hand. Then shrugging, she gave Chance a barely tolerant look before turning back to Wyatt. "Can't say I'm surprised." She sighed loudly. Exactly the way she would have before they'd started working together on this job. "Your brother has never had particularly *good* manners."

That had been true, up to now, when it came to Molly. That was going to change. Because now they'd stopped quarreling long enough to kiss, he couldn't imagine being anything but a complete Texas gentleman around her.

Wyatt exhaled in frustration. "Fine." He swung back around to Chance, growling as Chance popped what was left of his breakfast into his mouth. "Where did you get it then? 'Cause I don't remember Sage making German bread at her coffee shop in town."

Quickly, Chance shut down that line of inquiry. His only sister was worse than his mother when it came to interfering in his love life.

"Wasn't there," he confirmed.

"Then where was it?" Wyatt persisted hungrily.

Molly stepped between the two brothers. She interjected, "Maybe he made it?"

Wyatt shook his head. "Nah. I don't think so." He squinted, about to deliver another round of questions.

Figuring Molly'd had enough amusement at his expense for one morning, Chance lifted a hand. "If you must know, it was a holiday gift from someone I do business with. Okay? Happy now?" Ignoring Wyatt, he turned to Molly. "You ready to go over the project financials...make sure we're still on budget?"

Her reply was cut off by the loud *thump-thump-thump-thump* of a helicopter approaching overhead.

This wasn't an uncommon sight. A lot of wealthy people had homes in or around Laramie. They often flew in and out of the local airstrip either via private jet or chopper. The hospital used air ambulances, too. But this chopper was flying incredibly low. And coming right toward the Circle H.

While the momma cow and her baby bull hurried for cover in a strand of faraway trees, the chopper hovered over a large pasture, currently empty of livestock, and slowly, noisily set down. The motor slowed, then cut, the gusts of air fading.

"What the...?" Chance and Wyatt murmured in unison. The door to the chopper opened. And just like that, Chance was taken back to a time and place he had never wanted to revisit.

FEELING EVERY BIT as stunned as the two men beside her, Molly watched as a fiftysomething woman in a long white fur coat and ostrich boots stepped out. The silvery blonde was followed by a tall, lanky man in chinos, a sweater, a black leather biker jacket and sneakers. He had a decidedly unathletic air and appeared to be in his early forties. Last out was a thin, sophisticated blonde about Molly's age who looked like a younger version of the first woman. She had chic sunglasses over her eyes that matched her all-black clothing and body language that screamed indifference.

"Do you know them?" Molly asked, aware that the normally unflappable Chance seemed more perturbed than the unexpected landing should have made him.

Nodding at the approaching trio, Wyatt leaned over and quipped in Molly's ear, "The lady in fur is Babs Holcombe, Chance's would-have-been-mother-in-law-from-hell."

Oh, dear.

"And his ex, Delia Holcombe."

Who was, Molly noted, quite beautiful in that dissolutely wealthy way.

"No clue who the other dude is," Wyatt continued helpfully.

An unwelcoming look on his handsome face, Chance looked past them to where Mistletoe Jr. was cowering next to his momma. Sharing the concern, Wyatt touched his brother's arm. "I'll see to them. You take care of this."

Stopping just short of them, Babs looked at Molly. "You can leave, too."

Before Molly could react, Chance had an arm around her shoulders. "She stays," he said gruffly.

Molly hadn't been planning to. But…okay… if Chance felt in need of some kind of backup, she would provide it.

Watching as Chance dropped his arm, Babs said drolly, "Hello, Chance."

His scowl deepened. "Did you have permission to land that chopper here?"

Babs waved off any difficulty. "I'm sure your mother won't mind."

"What do you want?" he demanded.

Molly hitched in a surprised breath. In all their time together, she had never heard Chance be that rude.

"To introduce you to Mr. X—the founder of the X search engine."

No wonder the tall, sort of geeky guy looked familiar, Molly thought. She'd seen him being interviewed on TV. He'd also starred in commercials featuring the product that was on par with Google and Yahoo. One of the most famous new faces on the tech front, he stood to make much more than the billions he already had.

"Mr. X would like to purchase your bucking-bull business and Bullhaven Ranch."

Chance snorted as if that were the most ridiculous thing he had ever heard. And with good reason. Molly couldn't imagine the tech mogul running a rodeo enterprise. Even through proxy.

Chance's ex, who was lingering in the foreground, still appeared as if she wanted to be anywhere but there. Molly could hardly blame Delia. Coming here unannounced was a bad idea all around.

But Mr. X did not appear to know it. Grinning enthusiastically, he told Chance, "I've already purchased an alligator farm in Louisiana, a minor league hockey team in Minnesota and a salmon fishery in Washington State."

Babs explained, "He's aggressively adding to

and diversifying his business portfolio. And he's willing to pay top dollar."

Chance folded his arms, biceps bulging beneath his denim work jacket. "How nice for him."

Molly winced at Chance's biting sarcasm. Glaring, he continued flatly, "My bucking-bull enterprise is not for sale."

Undaunted, Babs handed over a piece of paper. "You haven't seen his offer yet."

Not surprisingly, Chance refused to accept or even look at it.

"At any price," he reiterated flatly.

Delia took off her sunglasses and rubbed at her temples as if she had a migraine. She gave her mother a sanctioning look, then stepped forward slightly. "Just look at it, Chance. Please."

"You'll be pleasantly surprised," Mr. X predicted happily.

Chance turned to his ex. Something painfully intimate passed between them. Exhaling, he took the paper. Read the number, shook his head. "Not for a thousand times that."

Before anything else could be offered, a powder-blue Cadillac drove up behind them and parked in the drive. Chance's mother emerged, looking coiffed and pulled together, as always. "Isn't this a surprise!" Lucille Lockhart said.

More introductions of Mr. X followed. Babs explained why they were there. Lucille Lockhart nodded agreeably. "Let's all go down to the bunkhouse, where I'm living now," she said.

Mr. X consulted his watch. "Actually, I'm not sure we have time. I have to get back to Silicon Valley for a board meeting this evening, and I really want to tour Bullhaven Ranch before I go." The billionaire frowned, impatient. "We could only see so much from the air."

Delia gauged Chance with the wisdom of an old friend. "I don't think it's going to happen."

Her mother sent Delia a swift, censoring glance, which seemed to deflate the young woman's spirit, before flashing a triumphant smile Chance's way. "Never say never!" Babs murmured, linking arms with Lucille. "But you're right. We do have some catching up to do first..."

Or in other words, Molly thought, Babs was planning to use Lucille to pressure her son into cooperating.

At Lucille's cheerful urging, the trio climbed into her Cadillac while the chopper pilot appeared to get comfortable in the aircraft. In the distance, Wyatt could be seen herding the momma cow and her calf toward the safety of the barn.

Chance was already bolting for his pickup, which made Molly wonder if he and Delia were really over or not. Every feminine instinct she had told her there was definitely some fragile connection remaining. What, precisely, she didn't know. Nor did she understand why it mattered so much to her what that connection was based on. Anger? Lust? Regret? It wasn't as if she were jealous or anything...

"I have to go check on Bullhaven," Chance called to her. "Make sure their flyover inspection didn't cause any ruckus there."

Molly hurried to catch up with him. "What about going over the financials on the project as we planned?"

He made an offhand gesture. "I'm not doing it here with Babs and crew still in the vicinity."

She could hardly blame him for that. She resisted the urge to compassionately squeeze his arm. Stepping away, she asked, "Where then?"

His gaze skimmed her face. "My place. Unless you want to wait until later today or tomorrow?"

"No. It really needs to be done ASAP." She headed for her vehicle. "I'll follow you over."

BY THE TIME Molly got out of her SUV, Chance was already talking to his hired hands.

"Everything okay?" she asked when he joined her in the parking area adjacent to the garage.

"Yeah. Luckily, none of the bulls had been put

out to pasture yet. So they were all in the barns when the helicopter flew over."

"That's good."

"No kidding." Chance compressed his lips and ran a hand through his thick chestnut hair. "If any of them had been spooked…"

Molly wouldn't want to be around to see the fallout from that. "So where did you want to go over the project statistics to date?" she asked. She'd seen a small office in the barn.

"Ranch house."

Molly nodded. That was her choice, too. It'd be more comfortable, and they were less likely to have interruptions from his hired hands.

Although she had viewed his home the day she'd driven over to talk to him about Braden, she had never been inside the sprawling log-cabin ranch house.

It was just as she would have expected. Big, open living area with a cathedral ceiling and massive fieldstone fireplace. Finished interior walls that were light enough to soak in the sun pouring in from the plentiful windows. Dark trim and wide-plank floors that matched the arching beams overhead. Leather furniture.

Chance strode to the kitchen, which bore a remarkable resemblance to the one he'd wanted to install for his mother in the Circle H.

He shrugged off his denim jacket and went to the sink. Rolled up his sleeves and lathered up to his elbows with gusto. "Can I get you something?" He rinsed his powerful forearms one at a time. "Coffee? *Stollen?*"

How about you? she thought, then pushed the forbidden notion away. Just because they'd spent a pleasurable afternoon together and kissed did not mean they needed to pursue the attraction.

A little flirtatious banter, however, wouldn't harm anything. "Really?" she teased, splaying a hand playfully across her chest. "You'd share with me?" 'Cause he sure hadn't been willing to share with his rancher brother.

He gave her an audacious wink. "You're cuter than Wyatt. Have better manners, too."

Her heartbeat picking up, Molly circled around to the other side of the island. Maybe banter wasn't such a good idea.

"Good to know."

He opened the well-stocked fridge, peered inside. "Juice?"

Since he was already pouring some for himself, she said, "Sure." Her throat was feeling a little dry. Their fingers brushed as he handed her the drink. Molly ignored the tingling sensation. "So…" She cleared her throat. "About you and Delia."

He cocked a brow. Turned, let his glance drift over her lazily. "I was wondering how long it would take you to get around to that."

Promising herself that her interest was purely that of a friend, and in no way meant to protect her heart, Molly savored the sweet-tart apple juice. She tilted her head, and their glances clashed once again. He hadn't shaved that morning, and the stubble lining his jaw gave him a ruggedly handsome look. "How long ago were the two of you an item?"

More to the point, is there any chance the two of you will ever reunite? Because if there was one thing Molly did not want, it was to be involved in a love triangle again. He quaffed his juice in a single gulp, then poured some more.

"We ended our relationship three and a half years ago."

Molly took her laptop computer out of her bag and set in on the counter. "Delia's mother seems bitter about it."

Chance sent her a bemused look, retrieved his laptop and set it on the counter. Then he sat down next to her. "Babs is all about accruing more money."

"So?"

"She didn't like the fact that my parents decided too much money would be the ruin of their children, and instead bequeathed us each property in Laramie County, where my parents had both grown up."

Trying not to think how cozy it felt, being with him like this, Molly forced herself to recollect the facts she knew about the Lockharts. "Sage got a bakery and an apartment in town. Garrett was gifted a Victorian and an office building in Laramie that now houses the Lockhart Foundation headquarters and West Texas Warrior Assistance. You and your other two brothers received ranches. And your parents bought the Circle H, your mom's childhood home, for the two of them."

"Right. The rest of the wealth my parents had amassed over the years—and there was a lot of it since my dad started and ran a very successful hedge fund—went into the Lockhart Foundation."

"Which originally operated out of Dallas."

Proudly, Chance said, "The charity helped over one hundred nonprofits until roughly half of the funds were embezzled."

Molly let out a slow breath. "I remember that,"

she said sympathetically. "It was all over the news last summer."

The family had been trashed for weeks before eventually being vindicated by the embezzler's daughter, Adelaide Smythe.

Chance shifted in his seat, the hardness of his knee briefly brushing hers in the process. "Since then, it's become a much smaller organization, with my brother Garrett as CEO. Although my mother is building it up again with constant fund-raising, the upcoming Open House being her largest effort yet."

Molly nodded. The two of them got up simultaneously to move their stools a little farther apart, so crowding wouldn't be an issue. She climbed back on her stool. "That's all very meaningful and noble. Why didn't Babs understand that?" Weren't the truly wealthy supposed to be into philanthropy, too?

For a moment, she thought Chance wouldn't answer. Then something shifted in his expression. As if there was a chink in his armor. Exhaling roughly, he finally explained, "Delia and I grew up together. We dated on and off for over ten years."

That was a very long time, Molly thought with a pang.

"And were about ready to get engaged when my parents made their decision and it became clear that I was not going to be the multimillionaire son-in-law Babs had expected."

"Still, it was Frank and Lucille's decision to make."

"Not in Babs Holcombe's view. She wanted me to convince my parents they were making a mistake. And if I couldn't do that, then fight the terms of my father's will in court."

"You refused."

His jaw tautened. "Damn straight."

"Why?"

His broad shoulders flexing beneath the soft cotton chamois of his shirt, Chance sighed. "Because my dad was right. Too much money is more of a burden than a blessing."

Not in my book, Molly thought uncomfortably. *There could never be enough in the bank to make me feel safe.*

"And I wanted to be my own man and make my own fortune," Chance continued. "However much it turned out to be."

Their eyes met and held.

Noting the charcoal color of his shirt made his hazel eyes look more gray than green, Molly nodded. She valued her independence, too. Unable to help herself, she touched his arm gently. "I can understand and respect that."

Chance caught her hand before she could draw it away and turned it over. Tracing the lines on her palm with his fingertip, he exhaled, admitting, "Initially, Delia did, too. Until her mother convinced her that she would never be able to be happy with a struggling cowboy on what was then a broken-down ranch." He dropped her hand and sat back. "So Delia ended it, and that was that."

Molly felt bereft from the absence of his touch.

She kept her eyes on Chance. "Except now Delia and Babs are back."

He got to his feet and walked over to the coffeemaker. "Only because Delia is part of the business sales and acquisitions company her mom owns. And Mr. X is a pretty big fish."

And recently single, if the gossip mags were correct about him getting dumped by a famous Hollywood actress who wanted a "less nerdy" beau.

Molly watched Chance put a paper liner in the filter. "Do you think Babs is trying to matchmake Mr. X and Delia?" Otherwise, what reason could there have been to have the recalcitrant Delia along? She certainly hadn't been actively trying to sell anything.

"A billionaire and her only child?" Chance opened a bag of dark roast coffee. "Oh yeah."

Restless, Molly got up and walked over to the windows overlooking his backyard. Neatly fenced pastures as far as the eye could see. "Then why bring Mr. X here, if that was Babs's goal? Surely there are other ranches they could have shown Mr. X." *Without running into you*, Molly thought a little jealously.

"True. But…" Chance added cold water to the machine. "Bullhaven is the best bucking-bull outfit in Texas."

Molly folded her arms in front of her, recalling the way Chance and Delia had looked at each other at the end of the meeting. There'd been a lot of residual emotion between them. Not attraction, but something she couldn't quite put her finger on. "It seems like there's more to it than that," she insisted stubbornly. Wishing, once again, that he would be more forthcoming.

Chance squinted. "Like what?"

Molly shrugged as the tantalizing fragrance of fresh-brewed coffee filled the room. "Maybe Babs wants to use your studly presence."

The rich sound of Chance's laughter filled the room. "Studly?"

Molly flushed. "You know what I mean."

"Yeah." He waggled his brows suggestively,

ambling closer. Cupping her shoulders lightly, he gazed down at her. "And I'd like to know more."

The last thing Molly wanted was to find herself in the midst of a resurrected love affair. She'd made enough of a mess of things falling for Braden's daddy without first making damn certain Aaron wasn't romantically entangled with anyone else. No way was she doing that again.

She drew a breath. "Is it possible that Babs is trying to use your past relationship with Delia to make Mr. X jealous and realize if he doesn't act—and soon—in pursuing her gorgeous single daughter that someone else, like you, will?" And if that were the case, was it possible something could be reignited between Chance and Delia? Even if only for a short time?

Chance cut off her speculating with a resolute shake of his head. "Not going to happen."

Molly propped her hands on her hips, trying not to notice how masculine and undeniably sexy Chance looked in the sunlight pouring in through the abundant windows.

Unexpected emotion simmering inside her, she pressed the issue. "You're saying there is no reason for Mr. X to be worried about you and Delia? You don't feel anything for her?"

Chance's gaze sifted leisurely over her face, lingering on her lips, before returning slowly to her eyes. "I feel pity."

Now they were getting somewhere, Molly thought, still feeling as if she were pulling oil out of shale. Tingling all over, for no reason she could figure, she demanded, "Why?"

"She's never been able to stand up to her overbearing mother."

And there it was, the trademark chivalry of the Lockhart men. The same chivalry that had brought Chance to her and Braden's rescue at the cafeteria on Thanksgiving Day.

"You wanted to help Delia do that when you were together?" she guessed.

"Initially, yes." Looking as if he wouldn't

want to be anywhere else, he lounged against the kitchen island, watching as Molly went back to their "temporary work area" and powered up her computer. "But eventually I realized Delia had to do that on her own."

Too restless to sit down again just yet, Molly curved her hands around the back of the counter stool, and asked, "What does Delia feel for you?"

Lifting one broad shoulder in an indolent shrug, he came toward her. "No clue."

"You don't want to know?"

She caught her breath as he neared. He shook his head, serious now; whatever initial irritation he'd had at seeing his ex again had faded completely. Now he was focused solely on Molly. And that focus was causing all sorts of chaos deep inside her. "What Delia and I had is over," he informed her, his voice a sexy rumble.

Molly wanted to believe that, just like she wanted to be rich. In money and family and love. "But if…"

"Molly." His impatience mounting, Chance

gave her a look of pure masculine need. "There's only one woman I'm interested in," he told her, taking her in his arms and pulling her flush against him. "And that woman is you."

Chapter Five

Chance could see Molly didn't believe him. So he did the only thing he could to convince her. He lowered his head and, ignoring her soft gasp, covered her lips with his.

She resisted at first, splaying her hands across his chest, but his instinct was to deepen the kiss.

Claim her as his. The need to protect her triumphed. He lifted his head enough to look into her eyes. The mixture of desire and need told him all he wanted to know.

The two of them had been destined for this

moment, from the first time they'd laid eyes on each other two years before. All the quarrelling and mistrust had been nothing but a prelude to what was turning out to be a magical Christmas season.

"Let me love you," he whispered, kissing her cheek, her temple, the sensitive spot just beneath her ear. His body hardened as he felt her quiver.

She lifted her face to his, then looked at him with all the yearning he had imagined she felt and knew he experienced. Then kissed him back with a sensuality that further rocked his world. Her hands slid around his waist, and she pressed intimately against him. Her moan of compliance was as blissful as her touch. "Only if you promise it'll be a no-strings-attached kind of thing."

Was she that kind of woman? He didn't think so, even as her soft, pliant body surrendered against his. But if she needed to believe so… "Whatever you want, darlin'," he promised, heartbeat quickening. "Starting now."

He swept her up into his arms and carried her

down the hall to his bedroom. He laid her gently on the rumpled sheets, then followed her down. The kissing resumed, deep and evocative, every fantasy he'd had fulfilled. Molly moaned low in her throat. His body hardened all the more.

He pushed the edges of her sweater up, drew it over her head and reached behind her to unfasten her bra. Her nipples peaked into rosy buds of arousal. Cupping the silky globes with both hands, he drew first one, then the other into his mouth. She put her hands in his hair, holding him close, and arched against him as if she never wanted to let him go.

Loving her response, he lifted his head. Unbuttoned the clasp of her belt. Feeling intoxicated by her nearness, by the fact she was finally... *finally*...about to be his, he asked, "More?"

Cheeks and eyes flushed with excitement, she smiled. "Even better, cowboy. Free rein."

"Exactly what I wanted to hear." Pure male satisfaction pouring through him, he paused to tug off her boots, then drew the zipper down and eased her jeans down her long, lissome legs.

Her bikini panties were made of silk. "Nice…" He slid his fingers beneath, finding the soft, damp nest. "But not as nice as this," he said, kissing her through the cloth until her back arched off the bed.

"Nice doesn't begin to cover this." Molly whimpered, uttering a strangled sigh that drove him wild.

The truth was, she thought, tangling her hands in his hair and hauling him close, she had never felt so cherished and adored. So completely overpowered by what was happening between them. And they had barely gotten started.

"But we're getting ahead of ourselves here," she warned, wiggling free. If they were doing this, it was as equals. "I haven't done my part yet." Sitting up, clad only in her panties, she swung one leg over him. Once fully astride him, she shimmied down the hard, masculine length of him, kissing everywhere she passed, admiring his broad shoulders and muscular chest.

He was so strong and virile. And willing to let her take them wherever she wanted, however she wanted. Grinning, she paused to kiss the burgeoning arousal beneath his jeans, through the cloth, then moved lower still. Taking off his boots. Moving back up to unbutton his shirt. He lay quietly, a complicit smile on his handsome face. Catching her hand, he kissed the back of it. "I could get used to this."

So could she.

Not sure she should tell him that—at least not yet anyway—she opened the buttons on his shirt, drew it, and the T-shirt beneath, off. His chest was as sleek and powerfully muscled as she had imagined, with a sexy mat of chestnut hair that spread across his nipples before arrowing down past his navel to the waistband of his jeans. Her fingers followed the path, eliciting a few groans from him and a bigger thrill for her. Wow, did she ever desire him. Every inch of her was throbbing, pounding with the need to be touched, loved, held. But first...

"I've got to see where this leads." Sating her curiosity, she unbuttoned his belt. Undid his fly.

"Trouble," he muttered.

"Then it's my kind of trouble," she purred, slipping her hands inside his pants and finding the hot, hard length of him.

Their reaction was simultaneous. He groaned. She trembled with pleasure.

Eager to explore him more fully, she divested him of his jeans and boxer briefs. Her hands moved across his abdomen. Down his thighs. Upward. Caught up in something too primal to fight, she cupped him again, with both hands, and then bent to kiss the hot, satiny length of him.

He groaned again, on the verge of losing control.

"I think it's time you found a little trouble of your own," he murmured, shifting her onto her back. The next thing she knew, he had taken complete control and whisked her panties off. Hands spreading her thighs wide, he found her with lips and mouth and hands. Exploring. Adoring. Sensation spiraled through her, unlike anything she had ever known. She gripped his shoulders, urging him upward. "Now," she gasped. "Before I…"

"Patience…" he said roughly, sweeping past the last of her barriers. She arched again as he found the most sensitive part of her and brought her to the very edge. She quivered as his hands took on an even more intimate quest. She was close. Too close. Fisting her hands in his hair, she panted. "I want you inside me when…" *Oh heavens!* "…we…"

"You'll have that, too," he promised as a wave of sensation started deep inside her. With a growl of satisfaction, he pulled her toward him. And just that suddenly, her release came, her entire body melting in boneless pleasure.

He kissed her navel, still stroking the insides of her thighs. "Worth it?"

No fibbing about that when she was still shuddering with the aftershocks of a 6.0 quake. "Yes." She gasped as he palmed her breasts and took her taut, aching nipple into her mouth. "Heck, yes…"

Grinning, he slid upward and once again captured her mouth with his. "I aim to please."

No kidding, she thought, opening her mouth to the commanding pressure of his.

They kissed as he stretched out over top of her and brought his whole body into contact with hers. She could feel his erection pressing against her, hot and urgent. Desire welled inside her. "Now?" he rasped, pausing only long enough to roll on a condom, then kissing her in a way that was so wild and reckless it stole her heart.

"Now," she gasped, knowing she would hold on to this moment forever.

Hands beneath her hips, he spread her thighs and slid inside, penetrating deep. She couldn't get enough of the taste and feel of him, the confident and soulful way he merged his body with hers, the seductive, indomitable manner in which he possessed her.

To her delight, he seemed just as hungry for her. Intent on taking his time. Drawing out the unimaginable pleasure. He kissed her with the same insistent, tantalizing rhythm, letting her know how much she deserved, how much he wanted her to have. And then she was wrapping her legs around his waist, drawing him deeper, exploding with emotion, awash in sensation. With a low groan of pleasure, he followed. And together, at last, they found blissful release.

CHANCE ROLLED ONTO his back, taking Molly with him. A mixture of fierce physical satisfaction and raw emotion washed over him as he savored their closeness. He pressed his face into her hair, drawing in her scent, her softness, while Molly snuggled closer. Still wrapped in his arms, Molly tucked her face against his neck, her eyes closed, body still shuddering, her breath slowing.

Finally, she drew a deep breath, her body still pliant and molded tentatively against his. Lifting her head, she smiled and opened her eyes. "Well. Christmas sure came early," she drawled.

He laughed, relieved that the regret he had half feared he would see was nowhere in sight. "It sure did," he returned softly. He couldn't wait for the next round.

The picture of sated elegance, Molly rose, wrapping the sheet around her midriff. She ran a hand through the mussed layers of her hair, then bent to gather up her clothes, giving him a fine view of her curvaceous backside in the process. "It's too bad it can't happen again."

Whoa. He had definitely missed something here. "What do you mean?"

Looking as if she suddenly found his bedroom too intimate for comfort, she disappeared into the adjacent bath to dress. When she walked back out, she had a too-serene-to-be-believed expression on her face. "Once is a fling." She sat down on the edge of the bed to put on her socks and boots. "Any more than that is complicated." She paused to give him a meaningful glance as he got dressed, too. "And my life is complicated enough right now."

He could see that she wanted him to argue with her.

Persuade her otherwise.

Only she wasn't about to let him convince her. At least not in this moment. "You're right," he fibbed, putting on his boots, too.

She stood. "I am?" Skepticism rang in her sweetly pitched voice.

Aware two could play at this game—and that's all it was, a game—he shrugged. "You're moving to Dallas." *Unless I can work a holiday miracle.*

She brushed by him in a drift of the lavender perfume she favored. "Exactly."

He fell into step behind her. "It's a phenomenally busy time of year."

She shot him a look over her shoulder as she glided down the hall with womanly ease.

"And the holidays are always ridiculously sentimental."

Which makes Christmastime all the more perfect for finding someone, he thought. Aware she likely did not want to hear that, either, he watched her rummage through her shoulder bag. "And you have a son to care for."

Molly plucked out a lip balm and smoothed some over her kiss-swollen lips. Finished, she pressed her lips together to set the soft gloss. Dropping it back into her purse, she brought out a brush and began running it through her soft auburn curls. Although she looked much neater now, she still glowed from the inside out. Anyone who knew her, seeing her, would know she had just made love.

With him.

And though Chance liked his privacy, he wouldn't mind anyone knowing that Molly was spoken for.

"Not to mention," Molly continued, oblivious

to the serious nature of his thoughts, "a problem regarding Santa and a trio of bulls to solve."

He studied the color in her high, sculpted cheeks. Had she ever looked more beautiful than she did at this moment? "I have that covered."

"You think you do," she said skeptically.

Grinning, he closed the distance between them. It was all he could do not to take her in his arms again. "I know I do," he corrected her arrogantly.

Molly danced away. "We'll see about that."

Determined to make this the best Christmas she and Braden had ever had, he chuckled. "You bet we will."

Molly took a calculator out of her bag. "In the meantime, we still have to reconcile the projected numbers on the Circle H renovation project with the actual costs thus far."

Another thing they had in common. They both took the success of their businesses very seriously.

Chance nodded. "Let's get to it."

An hour and a few cups of coffee later, Molly sat back in her chair and looked at Chance with amazement. "We've not only managed to stay exactly on schedule, we're fifteen percent under where we figured we would be in terms of projected labor costs."

He shared her pride in a well-managed project. Something that only happened when everyone came together as a team. "We work well together."

They did, indeed.

But apparently wary of reading too much into it, she said, "If this holds through the rest of the project, how would you feel about passing the extra revenue on to members of the crew in terms of an additional year-end bonus?"

Once again, the two of them were completely in synch. A miracle in itself, considering how much they had argued about literally everything a few short weeks before.

Chance smiled his approval. "I think it would make for a merry Christmas for everyone. And let's face it—as diligently as our crews have worked, they deserve it."

Molly smiled back and continued surveying him curiously. She moved her counter stool ninety degrees so she faced him. "Can I ask you something?"

He pivoted his seat, too. "Sure."

"How come you're still wearing two hats professionally?"

He nudged her knee with his. "You do the same thing."

She wrinkled her nose and took another sip of coffee. "Interior design and general contracting sort of go hand in hand. Bucking bulls and remodeling do not."

He reached for the thermal carafe. She covered the top of her mug, signaling she'd had enough caffeine, so he emptied what little was left into his. "Actually, they do. If I hadn't had the skills, I wouldn't have been able to remodel my ranch house or build the barns at anywhere near the cost I paid."

Molly powered off her laptop. Seeming as reluctant to leave as he was to see her go, she raked her teeth over her lush lower lip. "How did you get into both businesses anyway?"

"Construction was my first job out of high school," he replied, shutting down the accounting program on his computer.

Molly smiled at his screen saver—a photo of the retired Mistletoe being inducted into the Bucking Bull Hall of Fame. Their gazes met. "You didn't go to college at all?"

"My parents made me apply, and I was accepted, but I knew it wasn't going to work. I'm just not the kind of guy who's happy sitting at a desk."

Her eyes softened with compassion. "I'm guessing Lucille wasn't happy about that."

Talk about an understatement. "She and my dad both went through the roof. They also cut off my allowance and took away my car, thinking that would shake some sense into me."

"It didn't."

"I got a construction job and learned the trade that way for a couple of years. When I tired of doing that in the Texas heat, I went to Wyoming for a while. Lived in the high country and got a job on a ranch as a hired hand."

Her intense interest made it easy to confide in her. "That's where I learned cattle management and the rodeo stock business. And started saving up for my own ranch. But I also knew—" he stood and carried his coffee mug to the sink "—that goal wasn't going to be achieved in this lifetime unless I upped my income."

She grinned and joined him at the dishwasher. "Sounds familiar." She slid her cup in next to his.

They straightened, bumping shoulders in the process.

Aware all over again just how much he had enjoyed holding her in his arms, he let his gaze rove her face. "We do have ambitious natures in common."

"Sorry. I derailed you."

He tugged on an errant lock of her silky auburn hair. "You constantly derail me." *In a good way.*

It was her turn to laugh. "Go on."

He suspected he had better if they didn't want to end up in bed again.

"I want to hear how you came to be so good at ranching and building."

With effort, he turned his attention back to the conversation at hand. "Mostly by working both jobs simultaneously. I worked out a deal with my employer to help him with some home renovations, in addition to my usual duties as hired hand. I started saving every penny I could, took some business courses online and got my general contracting license." He cleared his throat. "I was about to buy a place in Wyoming and open my own general contracting firm when my dad got sick. So I came back to Texas, and my parents gifted me with Bullhaven. Then I moved to Laramie, and the rest, as they say, is history."

"Are you ever going to give up being a general contractor?"

"No. I like doing both. Plus, it gives me the cash flow to keep expanding my bucking-bull business without going into debt or taking on partners there."

He paused, happy to see she didn't think it odd—or unnecessary—to want to keep honing both skills. "What about you? Would you ever give up being your own general contractor on jobs just to concentrate on design?"

Her lips twisted thoughtfully. "In a perfect world, maybe. But I probably won't because having my own crew ensures the quality I want on every project."

"And control is important to you," Chance guessed.

Molly nodded. Returning to the island, she packed up her computer and then grabbed her shoulder bag. "Very."

"COWBOY CHANCE COMING? See me?" Braden asked hours later.

Seeing her son's excitement, Molly couldn't help but wonder if she was doing the right thing. He had no father in his life; Chance could easily fill the bill. If things were different…but they weren't.

She was moving.

Chance was staying here.

Hence, it was best to keep them in the strictly friends category, even if Braden—and the most womanly part of her—clamored for more.

"Doorbell, Mommy!" her son shouted, racing toward the door. Molly expected her heart to give a little leap when she saw the man on the other side of the portal. It seemed to do that a lot these days regarding Chance. However, she didn't expect the sexy cowboy to be carrying a rectangular folding table and three chairs. "Are we playing bridge?"

"Cute. Want to hold the door for me?"

"Whatcha doing, Cowboy Chance?" Braden planted both hands on his little hips.

Chance sidled past, being careful not to bump his cargo into anything or anyone. "I'm bringing in a present for you and your mommy."

"I like presents!" Braden declared.

Chance winked. "I thought that might be the case, buddy."

Unsure how this was related to their baby bull problem, Molly gave their guest a quizzical look.

"Patience," Chance said, setting up the table in a corner of the living room, well away from the tree.

He'd said the same thing when making love to her earlier that day. She flushed at the memory, all her girlie parts tingling.

His gaze raked her lazily from head to toe. With a tip of his hat, he said, "I'll be right back."

Molly and Braden stood at the door, watching, while he went to his truck. He returned, this time with a piece of plywood covered in sturdy white fabric, with cotton balls glued along the edges, and a shopping bag.

"Now I'm really curious," Molly admitted.

"Me, too!" Braden jumped up and down.

Carefully, Chance set the piece of cardboard onto the portable table. Molly wasn't surprised to see it fit precisely. He reached into the bag and pulled out a small colorful building. "Guess what this is," he asked Braden.

Molly read the letters on the front. "Santa's Workshop?"

"Right!"

"And some elves." Chance handed her son several figurines.

Braden set them down on the "snow"-covered board next to the building. Then ran off. "I get Rudolph and sleigh!"

The rest of the bag was empty.

Molly blinked in surprise. "No Santa?"

"Patience…"

Her body reacted. Again.

Flushing, she whispered, "You have to stop saying that."

"How come?"

She admonished him with a lift of her brow. "You know why," she breathed.

Mischief radiated from every fiber of his being.

Braden returned, the two toys Chance had already given him clutched in his hands. He climbed on the chair and set the sleigh and Rudolph next to Santa's Workshop. "I like this!"

Chance patted her son on the shoulder. "I'm glad you do, buckaroo."

Molly propped her hands on her hips while her son began to play with the four toys on the snow board. "I take it there is a method to this madness?"

Chance folded his arms across his chest. "There is. But for the next phase, it will require the two of you coming out to Bullhaven tomorrow morning."

Being alone with him, even with a small chaperone along, always seemed like a dangerous proposition to her way too vulnerable heart. She cleared her throat and lifted her chin. "Really?"

The corners of his eyes crinkled. "Really," he said just as firmly.

She stared into the hazel depths. "To do what?"

"See where and how real bulls live."

But was that all, Molly wondered, studying the sparkling invitation in Chance's smile, that he wanted her to see?

Chapter Six

Chance wasn't sure Molly would take him up on his invitation, even before she gave him a halfhearted, "We'll have to see how things go tomorrow morning… Braden can be pretty tired by the end of the week."

He knew that they'd made love too soon. And because of that she was every bit as determined to keep him at arm's length as he was to get her back in his arms. He also knew that she and her son were a package deal.

Convincing her that condition was more than

okay with him, however, was going to be tough. Fortunately, he knew, even if Molly didn't yet, that he was more than up to the task. And he was ready to prove to her they could have something more than dissension between them. She'd finally accepted his offer. Late Saturday morning, she drove up the lane.

He walked out to greet them. "Glad you both could make it."

"Braden really wanted to come and see all of your bulls." She emerged from the SUV and sent him a meaningful glance as she opened the rear passenger door. "And I got to thinking, maybe you're right, that it's a good idea for Braden to learn where and how real live bulls live."

He was glad she understood at least this much of his plan. "That they're only babies, pastured with their momma for a very short time."

She nodded.

"Hey there, pardner," Chance said, after Molly

got Braden out of his safety seat. He held up his palm for a high five.

Grinning, Braden fit his small palm to Chance's.

"You're just in time to see some bucking bulls get loaded onto a truck."

Behind them, an 18-wheeler headed up the lane.

Molly lifted her son into her arms.

The three of them watched as the truck parked just outside the barn. The driver—a husky, dark-haired cowboy in his early fifties—got out. "Three of our bulls are going to compete in a rodeo in Arizona next weekend," Chance explained.

Molly blinked. "They're leaving now?"

Noticing Braden was a little heavy for Molly, Chance put out his hands. Grinning, Braden slid into his grip. Amazed at how right it felt to hold the little tyke in his arms, Chance explained, "Bucking bulls can only travel ten hours in one day before needing to be pastured at night at one of the rest ranches along the way. And then they need an equivalent time to recover from the rigors of travel once they do arrive at the rodeo site."

Chance's hired hand Billy walked the first bull out of the barn. The sleek Black Angus had a name tag on his ear and, as always, was perfectly content to be led into the divided compartment readied just for him on the truck. "That's Kringle," Chance explained.

A second bull was walked out by Pete with equal calm.

"And Saint Nick," Chance said, grinning as the third bull was walked out.

"And last but not least, Dasher," Chance concluded as Braden waved merrily at the bulls.

Amused, Billy and Pete both waved back at Molly's son.

She turned toward him in a drift of orchid perfume. Was that new? If it was, he had to admit he really liked it.

"Are all your bulls named in response to the Christmas holiday?" Molly asked wryly.

His gaze trailed over the hollow of her throat, past her lips, to her pretty amber eyes. "You might say we have a theme going."

She shook her head, clearly not sure what to make of that.

Before she could say anything more, a ruckus sounded in the pasture. Noticing what was going on at the semitrailer, Mistletoe had crossed the grassy terrain and come to the fence. Looking straight at the truck, he lifted his head and let out another loud bellow.

Molly moved in closer to Chance and put a hand up to protect her son. "What's going on?" she whispered nervously.

Chance laughed. Holding Braden in one arm, he wrapped his other around Molly's shoulders. "Mistletoe may be retired, but he's still a prime athlete and he still wants to compete. He understands getting on a semitruck means riding to a rodeo, and he wants to go, too."

Braden looked at Chance, listened to Mistletoe and then let out a loud bellow of his own.

"Mist'toe," the little boy repeated, then again imitated the loud bellowing sound.

Chance and Molly both laughed.

Mistletoe looked in their direction and bellowed again.

Chance shook his head. "What can I say?" he joked as Molly, understanding they were in no danger, relaxed beside him. "Once a competitor, always a competitor."

The driver came over. Last-minute instructions were given. Papers signed. They all waved as the truck headed back down the lane. Mistletoe remained against the fence in disappointment.

"You want to know what might make Mistletoe Jr.'s daddy feel better?" Chance murmured.

"What?" Braden asked eagerly.

"A bath."

MOLLY STARED AT CHANCE. This morning was turning out to be quite a surprise. She had worried a little he had just invited them out to try to hit on her. However, she could see, given how much was going on at the ranch, she needn't have worried.

There was a lot more to him than an ability to make mind-blowing love and seduce her into tearing down boundaries and spending time with him. He was good with kids. Especially Braden. Kind. And fun to be around.

Had she not been moving 150 miles away, he might have been the perfect man.

If he hadn't also grown up wealthy, that was.

Aware Chance was grinning at her, as if wondering where her thoughts had drifted, she blinked herself back to ranching activity. "Bulls take baths?"

"Well, more like a shower, but yeah, they do."

Braden clapped his hands in excitement. "Hurrah!"

"This we've got to see," Molly agreed.

While she took charge of her son again, Chance grabbed a halter from the barn and went to get Mistletoe. As he brought his prize bucking bull back across the yard, he pointed toward a building on the other side of the complex of barns and training facilities.

At the end of the big bull barn was a cement-floored paddock that was the size of a drive-through car wash. The sides were open, but there was a stop gate along the back. The big black bull stepped calmly up to it. Whistling merrily, Chance tied Mistletoe to the steel gate, then went to get two folding chairs for Molly and Braden and a box full of grooming gear.

He got them situated on the other side of the stop gate, far enough away so there appeared to be no risk of them getting wet, then walked around to grab the long hose hanging on the wall.

"Do all bulls get washed?" Molly asked.

Chance put down the hose long enough to re-move his denim jacket. He tossed it on the grass next to Molly, then pushed up the sleeves on his light gray thermal-knit T-shirt. "All of mine do."

Molly's mouth went dry as she watched the powerful muscles of his arms and back flex beneath the clinging cloth. Remembering how all that satiny skin and sinew had felt the day before, beneath her eagerly questing hands, she asked, "How often?"

"Once or twice a month."

"Do you always do it yourself?" she asked.

"Pete and Billy help out." He turned on the water. "But I usually wash Mistletoe myself," he admitted.

It was clear, Molly thought, from the way Chance looked at the bucking bull that Mistletoe was as much a beloved family pet as impressive revenue source. Which went to show yet again how loving and gentle a man Chance was, deep down.

He wet the bull from end to end, then turned a dial on the handle of the hose and directed a sudsy stream into the hide. It seemed to work on the massive animal like a massage.

"Mis'toe likes it!" Braden exclaimed, clapping his hands again.

Chance chuckled and followed the soaping with a thorough rinse. "You're right. He does."

Molly leaned back in her chair as the fragrant smell of the soap filled the air. "When and where did you get him?"

Smiling fondly, Chance turned off the water and plucked a big brush from the bag of grooming tools. "My first Christmas in Wyoming. I was working at a cattle ranch, and one of the pregnant cows went missing. She'd gone off to give birth, got caught in a blizzard that killed her." Chance stopped brushing long enough to pat Mistletoe's head. "This fella was barely breathing when I found him."

Molly could only imagine how horrifying that had to have been. "But you revived him."

Chance sobered. His low tone took on a sentimental rasp. "Against all odds. Even the vet said he'd never make it, but if he did, my boss said, I could have him."

And Chance loved a challenge.

"So..." He got out the clippers and trimmed

some of the stray hairs around the bull's face and tail. "I spent the next few months bottle-feeding Mistletoe in the barn, seeing he stayed warm and healthy, and the rest, as they say, is history."

Finished, Chance dried off his hands with a towel. Pride radiating in his handsome face, he retrieved his phone and showed them more photos of the two of them in the barn. Apparently, Mistletoe wasn't the only one who'd been young and cute, Molly noted with an appreciative smile.

Chance turned on a blower to move the air through Mistletoe's sleek black coat.

"So now," Molly gathered, holding on to Chance's phone for him, "Mistletoe is the oldest of your bucking bulls."

"As well as a national champion and the sire to every other bucking bull I own." Chance patted Mistletoe fondly. The bull let out a low sound that seemed like the cattle version of a purr of pleasure.

Molly flushed, recalling when she had done the same beneath the caress of those large, talented hands.

"Mis'toe likes baths!" Braden noted yet again.

"Do you think he would fit in the bathtub at your house?" Chance asked Braden with exaggerated curiosity.

Molly saw where the handsome cowboy was going with this. It was all she could do not to applaud his subtlety.

Braden shook his head defiantly. "Mis'toe too big!" he declared.

"I guess you're right." Chance pretended to consider the matter. "I guess he'll have to continue taking his baths here with all the other bulls."

Braden spread his arms wide as inspiration hit. "Mommy build big tub!" He aimed a thumb at his small chest. "My house."

Molly had to hand it to her son. He had a talent for solving problems.

Chance squinted at Molly. "The perks of having a contractor for a parent?"

"Or a too-bright-and-imaginative-for-his-own-good offspring?"

In any case, they had yet to solve the quandary of how to convince Braden he couldn't possibly have a real live bull for Christmas.

Pete suddenly appeared. "Boss? There's someone here who wants a word with you."

Chance responded to the interruption with a lift of his palm. "Tell them I'll call them back later."

The hired hand winced. "Ah. I don't think she's going to…"

She? Molly wondered.

Please tell me I haven't made the same dumb mistake I made with Aaron, that Chance is not involved with someone else, too.

"Chance?" Delia rounded the side of the bull wash. She whipped off her sunglasses. "We have to talk!"

Of all the people Molly had expected to see

that morning, Chance's ex was not one of them. She started to rise.

Chance waved Molly back down. Then he informed Delia curtly, "Tell Babs the answer is no."

Delia put her sunglasses on top of her long silvery-blond hair. Once again, she was dressed all in black. "You don't even know what my mother said."

He nodded at the folder in her hand. "Is that an offer?"

Delia straightened, indignant. "Yes."

He handed the grooming box off to Pete. "Then we've got nothing to discuss."

The hired hand exited quickly.

Ignoring Molly and Braden, Delia moved imploringly toward Chance. She looked her former lover right in the eye. "Look, I'm not into chasing lost causes any more than you are, Chance. You know that better than anyone! But Mr. X authorized our firm to purchase your bucking-bull business for *well over* the assessed value."

Her words fell on deaf ears.

Chance unhooked the lead and began steering Mistletoe out of the washing area. "Maybe you and Babs should try showing him some ranches and rodeo operations that *are* for sale?"

Delia stomped closer to Chance, staying well clear of the bull. "He wants *yours.*"

His jaw set. "Then Mr. X is going to be disappointed," he predicted grimly.

"At least think it over." Delia pushed the folder at him. When he refused to take it, she shoved it into Molly's hands before turning and sauntering back to the waiting limo.

"WHAT DO YOU WANT me to do with this?" Molly asked Chance when the newly tranquil Mistletoe had been put back out to pasture and they'd retreated to the house for the casual lunch Chance had promised.

She couldn't help but notice that although there had been no yuletide decorations of any sort the day before, now he had a tree up and a wreath on the front door.

Had he done all that for her and Braden?

Or just simply because it was time?

There was no clue in the impassive set of his features.

Chance looked at the sleek black-and-white Holcombe Business Sales & Acquisitions folder and nodded in the direction of his desk. "There's a shredder over there."

Molly's jaw dropped. "Seriously?"

Nodding, Chance brought out what looked to be a brand-new box of plastic building blocks for Braden and set them in the middle of the living room floor. Together, they opened it and dumped them out. He patted her son's shoulder. "Have at it, buddy."

Braden settled in the midst of the toys, beaming up at their host. "Thanks, Cowboy Chance!"

"No problem." He rose to his feet.

Folder still in hand, Molly followed him over to his workstation. Keeping her voice low and tranquil, she looked him in the eye. "You're not even going to look at it?"

"No need." Handsome jaw set, he took it from her, walked over and fed it to the shredder, cover and all. He closed the distance between them and took her hands in his. "Why does this surprise you?"

Her pulse raced. "I don't know. I figured you'd at least be curious." She would have been in his place.

He dropped his grip on her and walked into the kitchen. "I know what Bullhaven means to me."

As always, his ultramasculine presence made her feel intensely aware of him. "There's no price for it?" she guessed, wishing he hadn't been quite so quick to let her go.

"No." He went to the fridge and brought out a package of hot dogs, buns and all the fixings. "I gather you don't feel the same way about your own home and business?"

Molly sat at the island, watching as he turned

the flame on under the stove-top grill. "I love the home I grew up in. I'm going to do everything I can to keep it as a retreat. My work will go with me."

Something flickered in his expression, then disappeared. "Any of your employees planning to move to Dallas with you?" he asked her casually.

Molly cast a look at her son, who was now happily stacking blocks. "No. But I've made calls on everyone's behalf. They'll all have jobs in the area after I leave."

He turned, his expression deliberately closed and uncommunicative. "You didn't call me."

She flushed under his continued scrutiny. "We weren't on friendly terms last fall."

"Ah." He moved toward her, throwing her off guard once again. He stopped just short of her. "Are we now?"

"More so…"

The wicked gleam in his eyes said if they were alone, he would have kissed her. And she would have let him. Luckily for them both, a faint chime sounded. Averting her gaze from his, she pulled out her phone.

"Expecting something?"

Molly drew a deep breath, glad to have someone to confide in about this. "A couple of things, actually. You know that special T-R-A-I-N set I had my eye on? It's all sold out. I can't find it anywhere online. And I've set up alerts."

He picked up a pair of tongs. "A knockoff maybe?"

"The reviews on those aren't nearly as good." Molly sighed.

The hot dogs sizzled as they hit the grill, quickly filling the room with the delicious smell of roasting meat.

He wrapped the buns in foil and set them in the oven to warm. "What else?"

This was a little harder to talk about. But she did need to vent. Molly rested her hand on her chin. "I was supposed to hear from Elspeth Pyle, the headmistress at Worthington Academy regarding an appointment for Braden. They're interviewing and testing prospective students and their parents next week. But so far there's nothing on my phone, or email, although something could still come via the postman this afternoon."

"You thought he was going to get one?" Chance asked sympathetically.

Molly sighed again. She knew she was reaching for the stars on her son's behalf, but she had really hoped. "Alumni recommendations are supposed to carry weight in the admission process, so the letter Sage wrote on his behalf should have helped."

His gaze narrowed. "Is that really what you want for him?"

Why wouldn't she? Molly ignored his clear disapproval. "The school is one of the very best in Dallas."

"Mommy?" Braden joined them and tugged on the hem of her fleece. "Hungry."

"Well, that's a good thing." Chance winked. "Because lunch is ready!"

Half an hour later, replete with hot dogs, chips, clementine slices and ice cream, Braden could not stop yawning. "I better get him home for an N-A-P," Molly said, leery of wearing out their welcome. Though, to his credit, Chance had been a very good sport about keeping up a nonstop conversation with her loquacious three-year-old son.

"No. Nap." Braden yawned again.

Molly figured he'd last maybe five minutes on the drive home before conking out. "You can look out the window then and wave at all the cows and horses."

Braden cheered. "'Kay!"

Molly found her son's jacket. "Can you say thank you to Cowboy Chance?"

Braden hugged Chance's knees. "Thank you."

Chance ruffled the auburn hair on the top of his head. Then he picked him up in his arms for a face-to-face goodbye. "You're welcome, buddy."

Molly accepted Chance's offer to carry her son out to her SUV. Though she knew it was past time, she really hated to leave.

She paused, her hand on the driver-side door. Then she said, "Seeing the bulls was fun, even if it didn't yet have the desired effect."

He looked down at her, his chestnut hair glinting in the sunshine. "It's early," he told her with his usual confidence. "Speaking of which," his eyes softened even more, "would it be too much for me to bring by another installment of the 'solution' this evening?"

Molly's heart leapt at the thought of seeing Chance again so soon. She also knew the faster they were able to adjust her son's expectations regarding the bulls, the better. Besides, it was Saturday. "Not at all. But come ready to work," she cautioned with a smile, soaking in his charismatic presence.

As long as they kept it casual and had a little

chaperone, their relationship would stay safely in the just-friends zone. Wouldn't it?

Molly smiled. "We're baking Christmas cookies this evening, too."

Chapter Seven

Braden answered the door at seven that evening, Molly by his side. Chance looked at the smiling penguin wearing a Santa hat on the front of Braden's knit shirt and the red-and-white stripes on his pants. "Nice pajamas."

Braden took in the second plywood board, covered in white, and folding table Chance carried in his right hand, the shopping bag of goodies in his left. His eyes widened in delight. "Mommy, look!" he shouted happily.

Molly wrinkled her brow. "You're going to spoil us," she said.

Chance winked. "Then mission accomplished. And by the way—" he let his glance drift over her cream-colored V-neck sweater and formfitting black yoga pants "—you're looking mighty fine, too."

"Then that makes three of us," she said, nodding at his green corduroy shirt and jeans. Grinning, she opened the door wide. A front had blown in since they had seen each other earlier, bringing gusting winds and taking the temperature down to freezing. Worse, it was the kind of damp cold that went right through your clothes. Molly reached past him to hold the door. "Come in out of the cold."

With a nod of his head, Chance obliged.

"What's that?" Braden asked as Molly shut the door behind them, once again sealing them into the cozy warmth of her home.

Chance winked at the little boy. "Let's see." After handing Molly the bag, he took the folding table over and set it up flush against the matching one he'd brought over the previous night. The white fabric-covered board went on top.

"We've got a North Pole over here, with Rudolph and the sleigh, and what is going to be a Christmas ranch over on this side."

"I like ranches!" Braden jumped up and down.

"Then let's build one, shall we?"

Together, the three of them set up a corral, a barn and a snow-covered ranch house decorated for the holidays. Three horses, a dog and a cat completed the menagerie. Last but not least were a number of snow-covered trees that could be placed on either side of the increasingly elaborate Christmas village.

Yet there was plenty of room for more.

"I play?" Braden asked.

"What do you say first?" Molly prompted.

Braden encompassed Chance in the biggest hug he could manage. "Love you, Chance!"

A lump the size of a walnut formed in Chance's throat at the unexpected declaration.

There was no doubt the earnest little boy meant it.

Chance knelt down, aware this was a first. "Love you, too, buddy," he said thickly, accepting Braden's joyous hug. In the foreground, he saw Molly, tears shining in her eyes. She needed a moment as much as he did.

Braden went back to playing.

Molly returned to the kitchen. She plucked an apron off the hook. When she had a little trouble tying it, he stepped behind her and did it for her.

He caught the scent of orchids before he stepped away. She was wearing that perfume again.

But then maybe she wore it a lot.

Maybe he had just never noticed.

"I guess this is what they mean when they say Christmas is for kids."

She nodded, her head bent over the handwritten cookie recipe on the counter. "Thank you for helping us with our dilemma, although I'm still not sure I see how that's going to convince him that it's not likely he will get a L-I-V-E trio of B-U-L-L-S."

"Patience," he teased. He saw her blush, just the way she had when they'd made love.

His body reacted in kind.

Aware this was no time to be going down that path, however, not with her son in the next room, he took an apron off the hook for himself and put it on. "We'll work it out."

Brightening, Molly put six eggs into the mixing bowl of her stand mixer and turned it on high speed. "Speaking of things working out unexpectedly...guess what I got shortly before you arrived?"

Chance watched her pour milk and baking powder into another bowl.

"A call from Elspeth Pyle, the headmistress at Worthington Academy! Braden has an interview on Monday afternoon. They'll give us a tour of the school at that time and also talk to me privately. Which means I need to take another adult along."

Maybe more than she knew if things went the way they usually did at the Academy. Casually, he volunteered, "I wouldn't mind going." For starters, it would give him more time with both of them. There were other things in Dallas that could be accomplished, as well.

As Molly zested the skin of a lemon, the bright flavor of citrus filled the room. She paused to look up at him. "I didn't think you were gung ho about this."

He shrugged, not about to enter that particular minefield and chance spoiling the evening.

A furrow formed along the bridge of her nose. She added softened butter to the whirring mixer, then sugar. "Not going to confirm or deny?"

He fought the urge to take her in his arms. "If you need someone, I'll be there. It'll give us a chance to take care of another matter while we're in the city."

She peered at him through a fringe of thick auburn lashes. "Like what?"

"I got a call from our tile guys this afternoon.

They said some of the tile for the kitchen back-splash was damaged or is not as perfect as you want it to be."

She frowned, already taking the matter in stride. "That's a special-order material."

"I know. I found some at a warehouse in Dallas, but I think we should probably take a look at it before we buy it, make sure the same flaws don't exist in that batch."

Molly nodded. "Absolutely." She paused, thinking. Then ran a hand across her brow. "This is going to put us behind, isn't it?"

He stepped closer. "A little bit."

Their eyes met, and he felt the connection between them deepen. "How come no one called me?"

"I told them I'd talk to you about it. Just in case you wanted to—" conscious of her little boy playing a short distance away, he mimed an arrow to the heart "—the messenger."

"Smart-ass." They all knew neither of them ever took any of their frustrations out on the crew. Mix-ups and snafus were par for the course of any building project. Molly took them in stride, just as he did.

The customer was not always as understanding. "Did you tell your mom?" Molly added lemon zest, anise extract and salt to the mixer.

Chance shook his head. He really enjoyed watching her move about the kitchen and work her magic. "I thought you might want to do that."

"I do, since it really falls on the design side. I'll see if I can get her to pick out something else as backup, just in case we don't have time to get her first choice and still make the Open House deadline."

"Sounds good."

She turned the speed down on the machine and handed him a bowl of flour. "Can you put this in, a cup at a time, while the mixer is still going?"

"Without making a mess?"

Her amber eyes glittering jovially, she patted his biceps. "I have faith in you."

He was glad someone did. He was competent in the kitchen but not a pro like her.

Still, it was nice to be included, he thought, carefully adding the first of what looked like half a dozen or so cups of flour.

He watched her retreating backside as she went off to get out the baking sheets. She looked good in jeans and skirts, but this was the first time he had seen her in something as formfitting as the black yoga pants. They hugged her slender but curvy frame with disturbing accuracy.

Whirling back around, she came toward him once again. Standing next to him, she watched him add the last of flour. As soon as it was mixed, she turned.

He cleared his throat. "So what are we making here?" he asked. When all he wanted to make with her was love…hot, wild love.

She smiled, oblivious to the effect she had on

his libido. "*Springerle*. It's a German shortbread cookie with a design stamped on top."

Feeling the pressure building at the front of his jeans, he noted with mock gravity, "Fancy."

She laughed, bending forward to remove the latch holding the mixing bowl in place. The V of her sweater gaped slightly as she moved, giving him an unexpected view of the delectable uppermost curves of her breasts and the satin edge of her bra.

His body hardening, he resisted the urge to take her in his arms, and instead, contented himself, watching her move gracefully about her task.

"It's one of those things that looks harder than it actually is." She picked up a wooden rolling pin with pictures carved into it. "Thanks to this."

"*Really* fancy."

She laughed again. Nodded at the other room. "Want to tell Braden that it's time for him to come and help?"

Chance gestured toward the sofa. "Ah, I think it might be too late for that." Braden was curled up, his favorite blanket beneath his cheek, the Rudolph Chance had brought him in one hand, a horse from his Christmas village in the other. "Long day?"

"Very." Molly unlooped the apron from around her neck, then set it aside. "I'm going to have to carry him to bed."

Aware he had flour all over the front of his apron, Chance took his off. "Want me to do the honors?"

Suddenly looking as if it had been a very long day for her, too, Molly sighed. "If you think you can without waking him."

"What's that saying?" He tilted his head. "Anything you can do I can do better?"

She elbowed him in the ribs, taking the joke in the spirit it was intended. "Just don't disappoint me, okay, cowboy?"

It was a casual request.

Yet one he wanted to take seriously.

"Never." He leaned down and lightly kissed the top of her head. Then after carefully picking her son up in his arms, blankie, toys and all, Chance followed Molly up the stairs.

MOLLY TRIED NOT to react to the sight of Chance gently laying Braden in his toddler bed. But it was impossible. The sight of the big, strong man tenderly cradling her son, and setting him down on the pillows, created an ache in her heart that was so fierce it nearly brought tears to her eyes.

Up until now, she had convinced herself that Braden was better off with one parent who loved him with all her being. Now, with Chance in their lives, even temporarily, she could no longer deny the truth. Her son needed a daddy.

He deserved one.

Had circumstances been different, had she and Chance been more compatible in all the ways that really counted when it came to long-term relationships, their future might have been different.

But they weren't the same.

He was the kind of man who could reject financial offers without even looking at them.

She was a woman who would upend her entire life to better financially provide for her son.

And money, she knew, was on the top three list of things couples fought about.

"Tell me you're going to let me stay around long enough to at least taste the *springerle*," he said when they were back downstairs again.

What harm could there be in a little more time with him? Molly wondered. Especially when the two of them were becoming such good friends. "Sure." Molly drew a bolstering breath and handed him his apron. "But be warned," she said with a playful look. "I plan to put you to work."

And work they did.

After rolling out the dough and then using the special pin to leave an imprint, they carefully cut and transferred the stamped cookie dough onto parchment-lined cookies sheets. Finally, it was time to put the first two pans in the preheated oven. "What about the rest of the dough?" Chance asked.

Molly smiled at the way he was really getting into the holiday baking. "I'm going to save that for Braden to do, first thing tomorrow morning." She covered the bowl and set it in the fridge.

"So now we wait," he said.

"We wait," she confirmed, her stomach suddenly clenching with excitement for no reason she could figure.

She liked cookies.

But she wouldn't empty the bank for them.

On the other hand, to be held in his arms again and or have another one of his kisses...

Hazel eyes glittering with a wealth of emotions she wasn't so sure she should decipher, he brushed aside a lock of her hair. "Have I told you how much I appreciate you having me here, with you and Braden?"

She laughed off the significance of her actions

and tried to harden her heart. "No choice really, given the ongoing live-bull situation."

Looking confident they would solve that dilemma, Chance wrapped his arms around her, pulled her close. "Oh, there's always a choice, Molly," he murmured huskily.

And the first one she had to make was whether she was going to let him kiss her again.

CHANCE SAW THE INDECISION in her eyes. Luckily for both of them, there was no indecision in him. He knew exactly where he wanted this liaison of theirs to go. Giving her no room to protest, he lowered his mouth over hers. She smelled like an intoxicating mix of orchid, cookies and delectable woman. And she tasted just as sweet, her lips as heavenly soft and supple as he recalled. Her body just as warm and although not quite yielding, not pulling away, either.

He slid a hand down her spine and back up again. Worked to erotically deepen and further the kiss. The move was rewarded with a soft, sultry moan and a surge against his body that had him hard as granite, and hungering for more. "Chance…"

Sensing she was a woman who had never been valued the way she should be, he wove his hands through her hair. "Just a kiss or two, Molly," he rasped, kissing his way up the nape of her neck, the sensitive place behind her ear. "That's all I'm asking."

And all, he was certain, she meant to give. She uttered another soft sigh. Wrapped her arms around his neck, rose on tiptoe and pressed her breasts to his chest. "Two kisses, then," she whispered, her eyes a dreamy amber as she looked up at him. "That's all."

Two kisses that would mean everything, Chance determined, savoring the way her heart pounded against his.

Resolving to make her realize how much they could have if she just gave them the opportunity, Chance resumed kissing her. Soft and sweet, slow and deep, and all the ways in between. He let her know with every stroke of his lips and tongue how much he wanted to be there for her, to let her know he cared. Enough to be as patient and gentle as she required, while cherishing and honoring her as she never had been before.

He kissed her until she was as caught up in the all-consuming passion as he was. And it was only then that he realized the kitchen smelled of burning sugar.

Molly noticed at the same time he did.

She broke away. Stared in dismay at the smoke coming out of her oven vents. Then jumped into action, as did he. She swiftly hit the power-off button on her oven and covered the vents with two oven mitts, stifling the smoke and cutting off the flow of oxygen before anything could burst into flames. Chance grabbed a chair, stepped up and undid the plastic covering on the smoke alarm just as the first earsplitting warning screech sounded for half a second, then abruptly stopped when he managed to disconnect it.

Chance and Molly tensed, waiting to hear if Braden cried out. Thankfully, only silence reigned.

Her face pale, she opened the oven door. The cookies inside were indeed burned black, but not on fire. With a grimace, she pulled out both sheets, carried the horribly smelling cookies outside and set the pans on the concrete patio behind the house.

He went in the opposite direction and opened a couple of windows at the front of the house for cross ventilation. Almost instantly bitter-cold air swept into the living area and wafted through the kitchen, easing the smoky smell.

Molly jerked in another breath, still distressed. "I'm going upstairs to check on Braden." She dashed off while he stayed behind. And as soon as the residual smoke was cleared out by the winter wind now gusting through the downstairs, he reassembled the alarm.

Eventually Molly returned. She still looked a little shaken but was composing herself quickly.

Aware how quickly the temperature had

dropped inside her home, as well as between the two of them, he moved to shut the windows. "'Everything okay up there?"

She nodded, her face flushed blotchy pink with embarrassment. "Braden's still asleep. No smoke made it up there."

He gave her the physical space she seemed to need. "Sorry about the cookies."

She scoffed and ran a hand through her hair. "I'm not."

How was that possible, he wondered, given how much work they'd put in?

Molly retrieved her baking pans and shut the door behind her. Back stiff, she carried the remains to the sink and dumped the contents. Whirling to face him, she lifted her chin. "I needed a reminder to stay focused. And not get distracted by this...attraction between us." She swallowed, amending half-apologetically, "Nice as it is."

At least she admitted that.

As for the rest...

She held up a hand before he could interrupt.

"I'm not going to lie to you, Chance. I enjoyed making love with you." She squared her shoulders defiantly. "But I meant what I said. It's not going to happen again. And this disaster here—" she indicated the burned-black cookies now filling her kitchen sink "—is evidence why."

CHANCE COULD HAVE argued the culinary disaster was not a harbinger of events to come, but the look on Molly's face told him their relationship—and it *was* a relationship whether she wanted to admit it or not—would be better served by giving her some time alone to sort out her feelings. So he called on every bit of gentlemanly reserve he had, bid her good-night and left.

On Sunday, Molly was "too busy" to see him.

He had a lot to do before he left Laramie, too. Including making hotel reservations for the three of them Monday night and an appointment with the tile vendor first thing Tuesday morning. He also arranged a surprise for Molly and Braden that he hoped would go a long way toward solving their "live bull" problem.

Unfortunately, when he went to pick them up first thing Monday morning, Molly looked more stressed out than he had ever seen her. Her son was in a foul mood, too.

"Something wrong, buddy?" Chance asked gently, figuring it would be best to talk to the little fella first. He and Molly could discuss whatever was on her mind while he was driving.

Braden crossed his arms over his chest, looking every inch as stubborn as his mommy. "Want my friends," he said.

Chance looked at Molly. She compressed her lips. "He knows today is Monday, and that's a school day."

Braden stomped his foot. "Go school *now*!"

Molly sighed. "I've explained we're going to visit another school this morning, one that's a little far away."

Braden dug in further. "No 'nother school."

Molly turned her glance skyward. "Let's just say he is not in a cooperative frame of mind," she said under her breath. "On this of all days."

No kidding, Chance thought. He turned back to Braden. "Some people like playing hooky."

Braden made a recalcitrant face at Chance.

"He doesn't know what that is," she explained, wringing her hands.

And there was obviously no time to go into it.

"Right." Realizing that Molly was probably nervous enough about how things were going to go at Worthington Academy for all of them, and further delaying their departure would not help that, he glanced at his watch. "Maybe we should just hit the road."

Molly relaxed enough to send him a grateful glance that made him glad he had decided to tag along and provide the much-needed moral support. "We really don't want to be late," she agreed.

At her request, they took her SUV. He drove. Braden fell asleep in his car seat soon after they started out. And they arrived in the city with just enough time to eat a quick lunch. Molly changed Braden—who'd gotten ketchup on his clothes—in her vehicle. A wash of his face and hands and a quick brush of his hair and they were ready to head for the Worthington Academy campus.

As they approached the glitzy private school, Chance shot Molly a reassuring glance, even as he wondered whether she would feel instantly at home there or completely out of her depth. And what either of those options would mean for Braden, or for the two of them.

GIVEN HOW MUCH research she had done on private schools in the upper echelon of Dallas society, Molly thought she would be prepared for her first glimpse of Worthington Academy. She wasn't even close. And hence, she could only stare as Chance drove through the manicured grounds at the Colonial-style ivy-covered brick buildings and numerous athletic fields, all with individual bleachers.

With the familiarity of an alumni, Chance pointed out the PE building that housed the indoor swimming pool and basketball and volleyball courts. Braden gaped at the students in uniform, walking in orderly lines across the quad. "It's even lovelier than the brochure photos," Molly murmured, impressed.

Chance nodded, his face an inscrutable mask.

"And you and all your siblings went here?"

Chance nodded as he stopped and waited for the cross-country team to run en masse across the street in front of them.

"Did you like it?"

Chance drove on. "Wyatt and I had a tough time with all the rules."

Not exactly a ringing endorsement.

"Zane, Garrett and Sage thrived." He parked in the visitor lot, outside the administration building. Paused long enough to put on his tie and jacket, and then they were off.

Elspeth Pyle, the headmistress, greeted them cordially. The slender fortysomething brunette was as elegant as Molly had imagined she would be.

She introduced them to the sophisticated silver-haired woman at her side. "This is Dr. Mitchard. She's our school psychologist for the pre-K division. She'll be administering the cognitive evaluation for Braden while you tour the facilities and observe an actual classroom environment. And this is Julianne." She pointed to a young woman who looked fresh out of college herself. "One of our tour guides."

"Mommy. You stay," Braden said when Dr. Mitchard attempted to usher him into the testing center.

Molly knelt down. "Chance and I'll be right back, honey. You just go with Dr. Mitchard and answer her questions. Okay?"

Braden's lower lip trembled.

For a second, Molly thought her little boy was going to have a complete meltdown.

But something in the confident, encouraging way Chance was looking at her son bucked him up. Braden squared his little shoulders and took Dr. Mitchard's hand. They disappeared into a room filled with toys and puzzles. Moments later, Molly could hear him chatting happily.

The testing under way, Molly and Chance were led down a hall, to the wing that held the pre-K classes. The doors had glass insets. A press of the intercom button next to the door, and they could hear what was going on inside.

In one, A. A. Milne was being read and animatedly discussed.

In another, the teacher was holding up large prints. The children were confidently and correctly calling out the name of the artists—Monet, Rembrandt, Picasso.

Molly was unable to help but be enthralled. Her son would thrive here. She was certain of it. And she would be able to rest easy, knowing she had made sure he started out life with every advantage.

To her relief, Braden certainly looked happy when she had finished her own interview with the admission counselor and headmistress.

She joined him and Chance in the preschool lobby, where they were seated in armchairs, side by side, engaged in some sort of nonsensical game that had her son quietly giggling.

Unable to recall when he had enjoyed another adult's company so very much, Molly smiled at them.

Chance smiled back.

Braden, Molly noted, wasn't the only guy really enjoying himself here.

"We go, Mommy?" Braden ran over and embraced her fiercely.

Hugging him back, Molly nodded.

Braden moved between them, taking her hand and Chance's. Together, they followed the brick path through the elegantly landscaped quad to the visitor parking lot.

"Good meeting, I guess?" Chance said.

Molly nodded. All her questions had been answered. "The staff was surprisingly thorough."

"When will you find out whether he's admitted or not?"

Molly jerked in a breath, suddenly feeling
anxious again. Aware Chance was waiting for
her answer, she replied, "The decisions will be
made by the end of next week, and all midyear
applicants will receive a letter via regular mail
the week after that."

Which meant she would know before Christmas. Would her wish for her son be granted?
Molly could only hope. Meantime, they had
what was left of the afternoon ahead of them.
Work on the Circle H ranch house that still
needed to be completed. And to do that, they
needed all the supplies.

"Do you think it's too late to go to the tile
warehouse?" Molly asked after getting into her
SUV.

Chance glanced at his watch. "They close at

six. With traffic, probably. But there's a place nearby that I'd like to show you."

Braden piped up from his safety seat in the back. "Want to play!"

Chance shot him an affectionate look in the rearview mirror. "I think that can be arranged."

"WOW," BRADEN BREATHED when they walked into the Highland Village Toy Emporium.

Wow was right, Molly thought, taking her son by the hand. The exclusive store was decorated for Christmas and filled to the brim with all the latest playthings.

A well-heeled older woman approached them, a huge smile on her face. "Mr. Lockhart!" she said, introducing herself to Molly and Braden as the store owner, Rochelle Lewis. "A little early."

Chance flashed a winning grin. "Not too early, I hope?"

"Definitely not!" Rochelle beamed. "We can take you upstairs now, if you like."

"What's upstairs?" Molly asked curiously.

Chance reached out and took her and Braden's hands. "You'll see."

They followed Rochelle through an employees-only door, up a set of cement stairs, through another big door.

Inside, the large area had been divided into three sections. Elaborate dollhouses with thousand-dollar price tags and play kitchen sets on the left, very fancy riding toys in the middle. On the left was the elaborate Leo and Lizzie World Adventure train set and all the accoutrements, which was sold out everywhere.

Braden, who couldn't have been less interested when Molly showed him the brochure, had an entirely different view when confronted with the reality of the fancy wooden tracks, windmills, stations, bridges and locomotive engines and sidecars. "Wow," he said again.

In addition to the basic components—which could have been located anywhere—there was a mini-set featuring the Golden Gate Bridge in San Francisco. Another that traveled through the

Grand Canyon. One with Big Ben and Buckingham Palace and the Thames in London. The Eiffel Tower in France. The pyramids in Egypt. Even one with the River Walk and the Alamo in San Antonio, Texas—a place where Braden had actually visited. Twenty in all, thus far. With new adventure sets coming out twice yearly.

"Take as long as you like," Rochelle said.

"I'm not sure showing him this is a good idea," Molly whispered to Chance while Braden moved a train along the wooden track, looking thoroughly entranced. "Given that we—I mean I—can no longer get even the basic components."

Chance shrugged with the ease of a man who had grown up with an unlimited bank account. "True, but the emporium has two remaining deluxe collector's sets left that include every item made to date. One of which is yours, if you want to buy the whole thing."

"They won't break it up?"

"Manufacturer won't allow it. Already asked."

Rochelle was back, price list in hand.

Molly took it.

And when confronted with the total, nearly fainted.

SHE HAD BARELY recovered when her son turned to her plaintively. "Want Leo and Lizzie trains, Mommy."

"I know, honey." She forced herself to smile, as the store owner trailed off to give them some privacy. "Aren't they wonderful?" And when the basic set did come back in stock, probably at some point after the holidays…

"Santa bring?" Braden inquired hopefully.

"Santa Claus has all kinds of trains," Chance soothed him. He was obviously more prepared to handle the situation than she was.

Braden got the mutinous look back on his face. "Want these," he stated, then turned and again began to play.

Chance stepped back. When she joined him, he whispered in her ear, "They have locomotive sets at the superstores, in a much less costly version."

But it wasn't the one she had wanted and now Braden yearned to have, Molly thought in disappointment.

"I checked. The other brands are in stock, too, so if you want me to go out tonight, while you know who is asleep, and take care of it for you…" Chance continued.

Molly drew a deep breath.

The store owner returned "I hate to rush you, Mr. Lockhart. Especially given how much your family has patronized our emporium over the years, but there are two other customers, standing by, ready to…"

Molly looked at the train set again.

Then the price.

With the kind of tuition she was going to have to pay at Worthington Academy, she just couldn't do it. "I'm sorry," she said reluctantly. "The deluxe collector's set is a little much for him right now."

Oblivious to the whispered negotiations going on behind him, Braden continued moving the train along the tracks.

"I understand."

Rochelle looked at Chance.

"I'd still like the stuffed giraffe we talked about for my nephew, Max," he said.

"Certainly."

Chance turned to Molly. "Mind if I go down and take care of it?"

Molly forced a smile. "No, of course not."

It would give Braden a little more time to play.

Which sadly, as it happened, was going to be as close as he got to owning a Leo and Lizzie World Adventure train set this holiday season.

"Sorry. I didn't mean to upset you," Chance said when they were leaving the upscale toy emporium.

She knew his heart had been in the right place. It always was where she and her son were concerned. She reached over and squeezed his hand. "It's good to have reminders why I need to work harder, bring in more salary, so that next year at this time, cash reserves won't be an issue." *A few of those jobs for Lucille's über-wealthy friends*, she encouraged herself silently, *and…*"I'll be able to do whatever I want, whenever I want."

Chance studied her, his emotions as veiled as his eyes. Once again, they seemed at odds.

Finally he said, "You really think Braden would know the difference between the high-priced versus the low-priced locomotive sets?"

"Before he'd actually seen and played with them? Probably not, but I would," Molly admitted honestly.

She could see she had disappointed Chance with her frankness. She couldn't help that, either, she thought on a troubled sigh.

He'd always had money. She'd never had enough. And like it or not, that created a divide between them that was not liable to go away.

Chapter Eight

Noting it had been quiet for a good twenty minutes now, Chance crossed the hall. Rapped quietly on Molly's hotel room door. There was a pause; then she opened it just enough so they could talk, without inviting him in.

"Everything okay?" he asked her quietly.

"You heard the meltdown?" she whispered back.

Chance doubted anyone on their end of the hall hadn't heard it. But figuring she didn't need to be reminded of that, he complimented facetiously instead. "Your son's got quite a set of lungs on him."

She cracked a faint smile at the joke. "Tell me about it."

"But he's asleep now?"

Nodding, she moved so she was no longer blocking his view, and Chance could see inside the room. Braden was curled up in the middle of the king-size bed, his favorite blue blankie tucked beneath his chin. His cherubic face still bore the evidence of his earlier tears, but he seemed to be resting peacefully now. Molly shook her head. "He finally exhausted himself."

Chance commiserated with the little tyke. "And no wonder. Given the trip from Laramie to Dallas this morning, the afternoon spent being tested at the Worthington Academy—"

"Followed by the trip to the emporium to see the toy trains, and the dinner out he really did not want to sit through."

Even though they had tried to make it simple and fast.

Molly leaned against the door frame, still keeping her voice low as she confided, almost as one parent to another, "Usually his bubble bath relaxes him, but tonight not even that did the trick. He just went into full temper tantrum. It was all I could do to get him into his jammies, never mind read him his usual bedtime story."

Chance wished she had called on him to help. "Tomorrow will be better," he soothed.

She looked doubtful.

Wishing he could take her in his arms and make love to her until her tension eased, he said, "Can I get you anything? Bucket of ice? I don't mind hitting the gift shop if you want juice or milk."

"That's really sweet of you."

Sweet was not exactly the way he wanted to be perceived.

"But I think I'm going to take a cue from my son and try to get as much sleep as I can tonight."

"Okay. Just so you know, though. My room may be a few doors down, but I'm just a text away."

"Thank you. For everything today." Without warning, Molly rose on tiptoe and pressed her lips to his cheek. She drew back and looked him in the eye. He caught her against him and kissed her back. At first on the cheek, gently, reverently, and then as she turned her face to his, on the mouth. Not in the way he had when the cookies were burning, but in a way that encouraged her to give him—them—a second chance.

Again, Molly drew back.

The yearning was in her amber eyes, even if she remained conflicted.

Yearning, Chance thought, was good.

Down the hall, the elevator dinged. Heavy metal doors could be heard opening. Voices, as other guests stepped off.

Aware he really did not want to push it, Chance reluctantly let Molly go. "Tomorrow then?"

"Bright and early," she promised.

TO MOLLY'S RELIEF, by midmorning the next day, Braden's mood was much improved. He handled their visit to the tile warehouse with his usual good cheer, and was still smiling and chattering exuberantly, as they all headed home.

"I like trains!" He lifted his hands high in the air, despite the constraints of his car seat safety harness.

Glad her son was so excited about Christmas, even if she had yet to exactly work out a solution regarding his gift, Molly countered cheerfully, "I know you do."

Braden kicked his feet energetically. "I like bulls!" he shouted.

As usual, Chance showed no worry over that issue. Which made Molly wonder what he knew that she didn't. "Mistletoe and Mistletoe Jr. like you, too," Chance reassured him.

Braden let out a joyous whoop. "Santa bring me trains *and* bulls!"

Again, Chance seemed confident it would all work out.

Again, Molly was not sure how.

Deciding, however, not to worry about it at this moment, when she had so much else on her agenda, she clapped her hands together and shifted toward her son, as much as her seat belt would allow. "Who wants to sing Christmas carols?"

Braden grinned. "Me do! Me school!"

Chance sent Molly a glance. "You're going to have to translate..."

Trying not to notice how handsome he was in profile, or how closely he had shaved that morning, she explained, "He's talking about the Christmas program his preschool is having. They've been working on the music for weeks now."

Chance looked interested. "When is it?"

Molly's heartbeat picked up. "December 18th,"

"What time?"

"Seven p.m."

"Can anyone go?"

Meaning you? "Yes," Molly said cautiously, her excitement rising.

"But?" he prodded, when she said nothing more.

She took a deep breath. Aware her son never missed a beat in a situation like this, she parsed her words carefully. "I'm just not sure."

He flashed her a sexy sidelong grin. "I'd be interested?"

Clearly he was.

In lots and lots of things.

Her.

Braden.

Kissing her again.

Maybe more than kissing…if the strength of his arousal during the cookie-burning incident was any indication.

Heavens, Molly brought herself up short when she realized the silence had gone on too long and Chance was clearly wondering why. What was wrong with her? Why was she such a welter of feeling and desire whenever he was around? She'd certainly never reacted like this before!

Not with Braden's daddy.

Not with anyone!

Except Chance.

"Because," the object of all her wildest fantasies continued persuasively, "I am interested, Molly. Very much so."

Swallowing around the knot of emotion in her throat, she tried again. "I know. I can see that."

"Then?"

She gestured inanely, wishing she were driving because then she'd have something else to concentrate on other than how ruggedly masculine Chance looked, even in a navy flannel shirt and jeans, or how good he smelled, like soap and sandalwood and man.

With effort, she babbled on. "Those programs are a lot to handle. Overeager parents. Way too excited kids." *And me, making a sentimental fool of myself, getting all misty over the slightest thing.*

Did she really want Chance to see her like that?

"Chance watch me sing!" Braden called from the backseat.

Chance smiled as if the matter was settled. "Sounds good, buddy!"

Braden clapped his hands. "Hurrah! Chance see me!"

They really had to get out of this loop before Braden invited Chance to anything else.

"Speaking of singing," Molly said brightly. "Here we go, now! 'We wish you a merry Christmas...'"

Chance joined in, along with Braden, their voices blending in if not perfect harmony, at least perfect good cheer. The sound of that and the other holiday tunes that followed was enough to warm her heart. For the first time, she wished she could stay in Laramie, and see where this was all going with Chance and still give her son everything he should have. But she couldn't. The visit to Worthington Academy had shown her that.

To do that, she was going to have to be all in—in Dallas. Not leaving her heart behind with Chance.

"Does Braden always fall asleep like that?" Chance asked twenty minutes later. The child had dropped off midsong. A check in the rearview mirror had showed him snoozing away.

Molly shot him the kind of affectionately rueful look he imagined mothers gave their babies' daddies. The one that said, "We're in this together."

And they were…

"Pretty much. Especially in the car. It's good though." As their eyes briefly met, he felt warmed through and through. "We have to drop him at preschool when we get to Laramie."

We. He liked the sound of that.

Molly thumbed through the calendar on her smartphone. "And he has a playdate with his best friends, Will and Justin, right after school, so I can meet your mother at the ranch house to look at the new tile we picked out this morning. Make sure she likes the way it looks in the light there before we take what's already up of the current backsplash down."

"I'm sure she will."

"I hope so," she said, her soft lips tightening anxiously. "A lot is riding on this job."

A lot was riding on a lot of things, Chance thought. He continued driving while Molly got on the phone with the crew working at the remodeling site.

He'd never considered himself that much of a family guy.

But then he'd never traveled with anyone like Molly, or anyone as cute as Braden, either.

He'd been cast in the daddy role and found he liked it. A lot. But then this holiday season was full of surprises, he realized, as he hit the town limits and parked in front of Braden's preschool.

Molly woke her son and walked him in, then Chance drove Molly home, so she could change clothes before driving out to the ranch to meet him and his mother and the rest of their work crews.

He walked her as far as her front door.

She rummaged for her key. "You don't have to stay."

"Don't want me to come in?"

She paused and looked at him in a way that said she did. "We're already running late."

And he knew if he did go in, they might very well be even later.

Putting his disappointment aside—this was something that could be picked up later—when they weren't rushed—he turned and headed for his own truck, which had been left parked at the curb. "I'll see you at the Circle H."

Smiling, she waved goodbye. "I won't be long."

He grinned back, aware he was counting on that. And much more.

"You look happy," Lucille observed, when he

walked in to the renovation in progress, at the Circle H ranch house.

He felt happy. Not wanting to discuss his feelings, he shrugged, and turned his glance to the work that had been done in their absence. "Time of year, I guess."

"Mmm-hmm."

"Don't read more into this, Mom," Chance warned.

"Hey." Lucille lifted her well-manicured hands in surrender. "I'm just happy you're happy."

"Who's happy?" Molly asked cheerfully, strolling in, too.

"Everyone, it seems." Lucille smiled.

Especially Molly, Chance thought. She had never looked better in a pair of designer jeans, cranberry cashmere turtleneck and a black down field jacket. Sexy. Competent. Warm. Kind. Feisty. Pretty much everything that was on his list for the perfect woman.

Oblivious to the direction of his thoughts, Molly asked his mom, "What do you think of the substitute tile we picked out, now that you can see it in person?"

Lucille viewed it from all angles. "I actually like it better than the original."

"Good." Molly's body relaxed in relief. "Then we'll get started on taking down what we put up, so we can go forward."

"Wonderful!" Lucille said.

Tank, one of the construction guys on Chance's crew, entered. "Express delivery service van from Dallas out here for you. Somebody want to sign?"

Chance bit down on an oath. *Not good.*

"I'll get it," Molly volunteered.

"That's okay." He moved around her, motioning for her to stay put. "I'll get the tile."

Molly shot him an odd look and dug in. "I want to check it out before he leaves." They'd taken the samples in her SUV. The rest had needed to be delivered via courier. "You can do that in here," Chance said gallantly. "The guys and I will carry the boxes in."

Molly gave him another odd look. "I can carry some."

"You really don't need to do this," Chance dissented.

Molly looked mutinous, but then Lucille stepped in. "Goodness, let's all go then."

They'd barely made it through the door when the delivery driver said from the back of the van, "Are the boxes from the Toy Emporium going here, too?"

Molly looked at Chance. He wasn't about to get into this here and now. "Those should go to the bunkhouse," he decreed quickly. "Mom, would you mind showing the driver?"

An old pro at social maneuvering, Lucille covered her confusion. "Not at all."

Molly peeked into the back of the van. "Are *all* those for here?"

The uniformed driver nodded. "Somebody's going to have a *very good* Christmas from the looks of it."

Except it wasn't a good surprise for Molly,

Chance noted, judging by the aggrieved look on her lovely face as she turned around, got in her car and left the ranch. It was more like her worst nightmare.

Lucille patted him on the arm. "Looks like you have some explaining to do, son."

And then some, Chance thought, wincing.

It would be better done without an audience.

MOLLY HAD NO SOONER gotten home than her doorbell rang.

Chance stood on her porch. "We need to talk."

She glared at him, not sure when she had felt so hurt and simultaneously left out. "Do we?" She didn't think so.

He brushed past anyway. Waited for her to shut the door behind them. Then shrugged out of his coat, his tall body seeming to fill up the space of her foyer the way the rest of him filled up her heart. Grimly, he surmised, "You're mad at me because I bought a train set for Braden."

Knowing she had to do something with her

hands or she would probably throw something at his handsome head, Molly went back to what she had neglected to do earlier—unpack her overnight bag.

Grabbing the handful of dirty clothing from the day before, she carried it to the back of the house to the laundry room.

"It's not just any train set, Chance. It's the deluxe collector's edition. The one with every Leo and Lizzie component ever made thus far. The one that costs more than some small cars!"

Brawny arms folded in front of him, he watched as she sprayed the ketchup stains on Braden's clothing with prewash, then tossed them into the washing machine. "As you once pointed out to me, it's quality stuff that will last for years. And could even be passed down to the *next* generation."

She threw up her hands in exasperation. "Please don't tell me you actually believe that!"

"Okay, how about this?" he countered, reaching for several pieces of laundry she had dropped.

Unfortunately, it was her red satin bra and bikini set.

He crumpled them in his hand, much as he had the first time he'd undressed her. "I wanted him to have it."

Snatching the lingerie from his fingers, Molly tossed them in the wicker basket she kept for unmentionables. Trying not to put momentary pleasure ahead of long-range goals, she tried again to talk sense into Chance. "I'd *like* Braden to have a lot of things, but this is way too much."

He lounged in the portal, gaze moving over her lingeringly, as if he were already mentally ending this argument by making love to her. "So let me give him some of it now, and then some more on his birthday and so on. Kind of like I've been doing with the Christmas villages, which, by the way, aren't finished yet."

Molly put two shirts in the washer, then realized they were navy and black and everything in the tub was white. She plucked them back out again, lest she get further sidetracked, start the darn machine and then have everything she washed turn an ugly blue-grey.

Deciding to leave starting the machine for later, she marched past him. "This is different, Chance."

He followed. "How?"

She removed Braden's blanket and Rudolph from the suitcase and set them on the sofa for him to find when he returned home.

Aware Chance was truly trying to understand now, she drew a deep breath. "It was one thing for you to buy a brand-new set of building blocks for Braden to play with at your place when you invited us to lunch. It made sense for you to have something for him to do," she told him kindly. "And you can use those for your nephew Max when he comes over to play." So it wasn't all for Braden.

"But?"

Molly could tell from the sardonic curve of his lip he still thought she was in the wrong. "This excess on your part just highlights the difference between us when it comes to money. To you, this is nothing. To me, it's a year of mortgage payments!"

He came closer. "If you are so concerned about excess, then why apply to Worthington Academy, where the tuition is more than some colleges?"

"A place like that will bring him boundless life opportunities."

"It will still cost an arm and a leg."

Ducking her head, she zipped the suitcase and reluctantly admitted, "He's applying as a scholarship student." Embarrassed to have to say that, because it made her feel like a failure, as a parent, to have to rely on charity to meet her son's needs, she rushed on, "The stipend Worthington Academy offers doesn't pay everything, of course. But it's *enough* that, if Braden does get in, I could afford it and then, hopefully, after a couple of years at a much higher income for me, he wouldn't even need that financial assistance to go there."

Chance spread his hands wide. "Look, if he gets in, I can help you with that—if it's what you really want for him. You don't *have* to rely on scholarship."

Molly carried the suitcase to the garage and stuck it on a shelf. She spun back around and marched into the house. Once again, he was using money—his money—to solve everything. "You're missing the point, Chance," she said angrily.

"No. You're missing the point!" Chance returned gruffly. "I did what I did because I care enough about you and your son to want to see you *happy*."

Tears of frustration blurred her vision. With trembling fingers, Molly wiped them away. "Buying us extravagant stuff won't achieve that!"

"Then what will?" he demanded, taking her by the shoulders.

Love, Molly thought.

Shocked by the notion, she shook her head.

Too late, he had seen the raw need reflected in her eyes. He caught her hand and pulled her to him. The next thing she knew he was sliding his fingers through her hair, kissing her lips, her cheek, her hair and then, ever so wantonly, her lips again. It was almost as if he were on a mission, not just to make her his but to give her every Christmas wish she had ever wanted.

A man in her life who would give her everything.

A man who adored her son as much as she did.

A hot affair.

Someone to share life's up and downs with.

He cradled her cheek in his hand. "Tell me you forgive me for overstepping," he whispered, kissing her hotly, thoroughly again. "Tell me you'll give me a second chance."

"To be friends?"

"To be a hell of a lot more than just friends." He slid a hand beneath her knees. Lifting her into his arms, he carried her up the stairs, down the hall to her bedroom. He had never been in there before. And she wouldn't have wanted him to see it now, with clothes draped everywhere. "Burglary?" he joked.

"Wardrobe crisis," she murmured in a strangled voice. *For the trip to Dallas. Because I wanted to look good for you.* Somehow she managed not to hide her eyes. "Don't ask."

"Okay if we clear a space?" He set her down gently on the floor.

"I'll help." Her sense of humor returning as quickly as her smile, Molly picked up an armload of garments and tossed them onto a nearby reading chair. He laughed and carried the rest over and set it on top.

The sheets were already rumpled. She hadn't had time the previous morning to make her bed.

"Now, where were we?" he asked her, easing his hands beneath the hem of her sweater.

"Kissing and making up?" At least that was where she wanted them to be. She hated fighting with him. Hated the thought that they might go back to what they had been, irritants who did nothing more than get each other's goat.

He grinned. "I think I can pick up there…" He gathered her close and lifted her face to his. Their mouths met, and she savored the feeling of his lips moving over hers. He kissed her like there was nothing standing between them, nothing but this moment in time. And it wasn't hard to stay in the moment, not when his hands were sifting through her hair, his tongue was playing with hers, even as the powerful muscles of his chest abraded the softness of her breasts and, lower still, his hardness pressed against her belly.

Something was happening between them, something that thus far had surpassed her wildest expectations. And she could no more deny it than the desire welling up inside her. Her knees weakening, her whole body swaying, she threw herself into the kiss. She ran her hands over his chest, unbuttoning his shirt, tugging the thermal tee from the waistband of his jeans. She smoothed her hands over the warm, satiny muscles of his pecs, finding out his nipples were as hard as hers. She kissed his neck, savoring the salty taste of his skin.

He did the same, easing his palms beneath her sweater, unfastening her bra, then smoothing his palms over her breasts. Quivering as he found the taut, aching buds, Molly lifted her mouth to his. And still they kissed. Caresses pouring out of them, one after another. Feelings built and desire exploded in liquid, melting heat. Unable to stand it any longer, they undressed. Quickly. Then joined each other in the mussed sheets of her bed.

He found protection, and she strained against him. Wanting. Needing. Pleasing. She lifted her hips. The hard length of him pressed into her. She had time to draw one breath and then they were kissing again, as if the world, their world, was going to end. Her inhibitions fled, and she arched against him, drawing him in.

He held her arms above her head. Timing his

movements, increasing her pleasure, then his. Building, probing, taking her to the very depths. Until she was clenched around him, gasping his name, and he was saying hers. They were racing toward the edge, spinning over, drifting ever so slowly back to consciousness. Then holding each other, kissing ravenously, they started all over again.

"I'M GOING TO WORK late tonight. Want to join me?" Chance asked an hour later.

Molly shook her head. "I have to pick up Braden from his playdate."

"I could come by later. We could all have dinner together."

Silence.

"Or not," he said.

Molly swallowed. Clad only in her bra and panties, she sat on the edge of her bed. Now that the lovemaking was over, and it was back to the normal routine, whatever that was, she seemed confused and on edge. And that gave rise to an unexpected insecurity in him, as well.

Molly paid an inordinate amount of attention to the act of putting on her wild purple socks. "Even with the nap he had in the car this morning, en route back from Dallas, it's been a really long day for him."

Chance resisted the urge to take her in his arms and make love to her all over again. Until she finally believed, as did he, everything was eventually going to be okay. "You want to put the little tyke to bed early?" he presumed.

Turning, Molly nodded.

"You want to put yourself to bed early, too?"

She trembled with exhaustion and something else. "I think so, yes." She flashed a weak grin.

He wished he were invited, but he could see it wasn't going to happen. Not tonight anyway. He rose and began to dress, aware there was one thing they hadn't finished. "About the Leo and Lizzie toys…"

Her eyes lifted to his. The turbulent sheen

was back. "I know you went to a lot of trouble, but I'm going to have to think about that. Let you know."

Another harbinger of trouble to come? Or just a necessary time-out? Chance couldn't tell. And he still didn't know when he got back to the Circle H. The guys were preparing to work late to finish the removal of the last of the backsplash tile that had already gone up. Chance told them to go on. "I'll finish it," he said.

"Sure, boss?"

He nodded. Truth was, he needed some time alone. Needed to be busy. Needed not to think about what would happen if Molly did what she was promising all along, and left for Dallas in January.

"THINGS WENT BADLY with Molly, hmm?" Sage observed, walking in, covered dinner plate in hand.

Chance looked up from his hammer and chisel. The lovemaking between he and Molly had been spectacular. To the point he was still re-playing it in his mind, and would be, he figured, all night. Molly's reaction afterward, the way she had pulled away emotionally yet again, had not been so great. But none of this was something he wanted to discuss with his sister, even if he could see she was trying to help.

"What makes you think that?" he asked casually.

"Duh. Mom told me how upset she was about the Toy Emporium boxes." Sage set his dinner plate down. "Sounds like you really blew it."

Chance kept right on chiseling off tile. "You wouldn't think that if you could have seen Braden's face when he was playing with those trains, the way he lit up. Plus, it'd be a great way to get him off the subject of expecting Santa to bring him a live bull for Christmas, if he had to make a choice." In fact, Chance was pretty sure it would solve the problem entirely. And hadn't that been the goal from the outset?

Sage settled on the sawhorse. "Look, there's

no denying your heart was in the right place, even if it was your stubborn attitude that got you into this mess in the first place. But you have to understand. To do all that on top of what you did to get Molly and Braden interviewed at Worthington Academy—"

A piece of tile fell out of his hand and shattered as it hit the floor.

Grimacing, Chance hunkered down to sweep up the shards. "Molly doesn't know I had anything to do with that. She thinks it was your alumni letter of recommendation that opened the door."

Sage paled. "If she finds out."

"She won't. I talked to Elspeth Pyle, the headmistress."

Sage paused. "Is Braden's acceptance a sure thing?"

Chance shook his head. "No. The decision, whatever it is, will be merit based. I made sure of that."

Another heavy silence fell. Finally, his sister got up to hold the dustpan for him. "What I don't understand is why you got involved with any of this elite private school stuff at all, Chance. Given the way you felt about your education there."

He took the pan and emptied it into the trash barrel with the rest of the broken tile.

Aware Sage was still waiting, he explained, "I did it because it was what Molly wanted." And he wanted her to have everything she wanted and more.

Sage settled on the sawhorse once again.

Figuring if he ever wanted his little sister to vamoose, he was going to have to eat, Chance picked up the plate and removed the foil. "And because up to now it's been more idealistic than real for Molly." He shoveled up a bite of tamale pie that was, he admitted, as delicious as everything else his chef sister made.

"In what sense?" Sage asked.

"Molly's a small-town girl from a protected environment. She hasn't had a clue what she would really be getting into, moving among those kind of people." He paused to eat a little more and let his words sink in. "I wanted her and Braden to see and experience it firsthand."

Sage went to the cooler they kept for the workers and fished out bottles of flavored water for them both. She uncapped and handed him his. "Did the tour of the academy discourage Molly the way you hoped?"

That was the hell of it. "No."

"So she may still be leaving Laramie County after all," Sage surmised, as unhappy for him as he felt.

"She's still got time to reconsider," Chance said.

Sage studied him, empathy in her eyes. "But you want them here with you."

He did. More than he wanted to admit. Even to himself.

Chapter Nine

"You've got company," Billy said.

Chance turned in the direction his hired hand indicated. Sure enough, a red SUV had parked in the drive beside the ranch house. His pulse picked up as he saw the driver-side door open. Molly stepped out.

It had been nearly seventy-two hours since they'd spoken. Although it had been hard as hell, he'd given her the space she requested. Hoping that once she thought more about it, she would see that his heart had been in the right place, even if his actions regarding Braden's gift had been—in her view, anyway—completely misguided.

"Want me to take over for you?"

"Yeah." Chance opened up one last gate. Jingle All the Way lifted his head and eagerly moved out of his stall into the bull exerciser. With all four slots filled, Chance turned toward his visitor.

Molly came toward him, a vision in a red wool coat, snowy white blouse, jeans and boots. That quickly his heartbeat sped up.

She inclined her head toward the circular slow-moving metal fence that connected to a long chute from the barn. "That looks like an open-air revolving door."

Chance closed the distance between them. Just as he had hoped, she was wearing that orchid perfume he liked. "Bucking bulls are athletes. They need to stay in shape." He pointed out the four individual sections that kept the animals apart. "The competition of following the bull in front of them keeps them interested."

Molly smiled and stepped even closer to Chance. "Pretty cool way to keep them in shape." She tilted her face up to his. "How long do they stay in there?"

"Thirty minutes daily."

"Impressive."

He quirked a brow. "That why you're here?"

"Nope. I need to talk to you. In private, if possible."

He wanted to be alone with her, too. As they headed away from the bull barns, and the attention of his hired hands, her soft lips twisted ruefully.

"I want to apologize for not being more appreciative the last time we saw each other." She paused to get a pretty glass container with a ribbon wrapped around the top from her vehicle. She had to lean across the driver seat to reach it. The hem of her coat rode up, revealing her nicely rounded derriere and slender, shapely thighs.

She inhaled deeply, as she straightened and faced him once again. Solemnly, she continued, "In retrospect, I see you were trying to help me achieve my goal of gifting Braden the Leo and Lizzie toys in a way that was impossible for me. So, if you will accept my peace offering of *Vanillekipferl*, or almond crescent cookies, I'd like to make a deal with you."

He accompanied her up the steps to the ranch house. Aware he was happier than he'd been in three days, he paused to hold the door for her. "I'm listening."

She scooted past. Allowing him to take her coat, she waited for him to remove his, then handed him the cookie jar. "I'd like to purchase the Leo and Lizzie World Adventure train table from you. The basic starter track set. And one of the destination kits from you. Preferably the San Antonio River Walk setup, since Braden's actually been there."

Tenderness spiraled through him. "The rest?"

"You can do whatever you like."

Then that was easy, Chance thought. He'd keep them for the future, to give to Braden, one at a time, on the holidays and birthdays to come.

Oblivious to his thoughts, Molly suggested, "You can sell the other components to parents who are still looking for them or gift them to your nephew Max."

Chance worked the lid off the jar and ate one of the cookies. *Delicious.* "He just took his first steps so he's a little young yet for the train."

Molly paused. "Right. Well, anyway, does that sound good to you?"

What was right was having her here again, in his home, meeting him halfway on an issue that was very important to both of them. He couldn't help but think that was a sign of more good things to come.

"I took all the boxes and put them in the spare room I use for storage. They're still in the shipping cartons, so you may want to open them so you can get a better look at what you'd be buying." There were colorful pictures on every box.

Molly's amber eyes gleamed. "Sounds good."

He went into the kitchen and got a pair of scissors for her.

Figuring he'd give her more of the space she had requested, then join her when she was ready for his company, he pointed down the hall that led to the bedrooms. "First room on your left."

"Thanks." With another grateful look, Molly disappeared down the hall.

Outside, a purring car engine halted. Doors slammed.

Chance went to the window and swore at what he saw.

MOLLY HAD JUST cut open the first box when she heard the feminine voice coming from the living area. "Stop being so stubborn, Chance Lockhart!" Babs's distinctive drawl echoed through the home. "This is a fantastic offer!"

"I told you," Chance growled back. "I'm not

selling to Mr. X, and I'm certainly not going to become partners with him!"

"Think of the capital he's ready to infuse!"

"Rather not, Babs."

Silence.

"If you do things Mr. X's way, you'd finally be able to make it up to Delia—"

"Mom! Our commission on this deal is not Chance's responsibility!"

No kidding, Molly thought.

"Wouldn't it be nice to finally be able to give Delia what she deserves?" Babs persisted. "Since you wasted nearly ten years of her eligibility, stringing her along, *pretending* to be interested in something long term, like marriage?"

Ouch, Molly thought. Although she could hardly imagine Chance pretending anything. He was usually as straightforward as possible.

"First of all, *Mom*," Delia cut in again. "Those weren't wasted years! Chance and I learned a lot from each other."

Chance's heavy footsteps moved across the

wood floor. "Ladies, thanks for stopping by. Next time—" the front door opened "—save yourself the trip."

Molly surreptitiously looked out the window blinds into the yard. A miserable-looking Delia was already getting into the sleek black limo. Her fur-clad mother was unable to resist one last insult lobbed Chance's way.

"And here I was hoping you would have gotten at least a little wiser when it comes to what is important in life." Babs sniffed, glaring at Chance. "Apparently not!"

Molly moved away from the window as the limo drove off.

She walked back to the main living area in time to see Chance feeding another set of papers to the shredder.

"You heard."

"Impossible not to. You okay?"

"Just frustrated."

"Why do they keep coming back when you've already told them no?" Molly thought about the lingering emotional connection she'd heard briefly in Delia's voice. Babs had to be aware of it, too. "Is Babs trying to reunite you and Delia via reverse psychology?"

Chance laughed mirthlessly. "I would hardly think so."

But there was something devious going on with the older woman. Molly felt it in her bones.

"The last thing Babs wants is her daughter on a ranch in the middle of nowhere. Even if the proposal she just hammered out would likely quadruple my income in the next year."

She did a double take. Unable to suppress her shock, she echoed, "Quadruple it? *Really*?"

He lifted his broad shoulders in a derisive shrug. "Sure, if I wanted to sell half interest in all thirty of my bulls and start aggressively marketing bull semen."

They were standing so close she could feel the heat emanating from his powerful body. "Why don't you want to do that?"

He walked over to plug in the Christmas tree.

The lights added a cheerful glow to the glittering silver-and-gold ornaments. Noticing the star at the top was listing slightly to one side, he reached up to straighten it, then turned back to her. "If you partner with someone on a rodeo bull, the partner gets an equal say in how often, when and where, you let the bull compete."

"And that's a problem because…?"

He opened up a tin of the dark chocolate peppermint patties he favored and offered her one. This time she took it.

"Partners can get greedy and think more about the bottom line than the health and welfare of the animal."

Eyes still on his, she ripped open the foil covering. "What about stud services?"

"Again, I prefer to pick and choose. Keeping the offspring genetically admirable keeps the price high."

He opened the fireplace screen. "Letting just anyone breed off your bulls can affect the quality of calves, and that in turn can affect reputation. And lowered reputations mean lowered prices." He added a few more logs to the grate, adjusting them just so. "Plus, I like the size of the ranch and stable I have now." He added tinder and lit a match. "I don't want any more."

Molly moved close enough to admire the leaping flames. "I can understand that. Sometimes independence is more important than more money in the bank." She stepped back as he closed the screen again and stood, too. "What I don't understand is why Babs is so fixated on arranging the sale of Bullhaven to Mr. X. I mean, I know that Mistletoe is a national champion, and you have an incredible reputation within the business, but it's not like she couldn't find another bull operation in Texas for Mr. X to invest in." She furrowed her brow in confusion. "And since he wants to add venture capital, too, and become a half-interest partner, he could easily find people with the skills to vastly improve whatever bucking-bull operation he does end up purchasing."

The brooding expression on Chance's face indicated this was bothering him, too.

Molly paused. "Is she trying to wreak some sort of revenge on you for not giving her daughter the kind of pampered lifestyle Babs feels Delia deserves? By either taking away or disrupting what she knows means the most to you? Your ranch?"

He grinned, his ardent gaze roving her upturned face. "You sound protective."

Molly flushed. She *felt* protective. Even though, technically, she really had no right to be that involved in his life. Given that they were simply friends—and temporary lovers—Molly squared her shoulders and drew a bolstering breath. "I just don't want to see you used by someone who definitely does not seem to have your best interests at heart. No matter what Babs tells her daughter. It's not right."

"Right or not, that's the way Delia's mother operates."

Molly squinted, her need to protect Chance

and everything he held near and dear increasing tenfold. "What do you mean?"

"Babs always has an agenda. Right now, my guess is that it has more to do with Mr. X than me, since it's his billions she wants for her daughter."

Molly took a moment to think about what he was saying. "So Babs is using you and your past with Delia—" *and Delia's residual feelings for you, whatever they are* "—to make Mr. X jealous."

"Maybe." Chance shrugged, not seeming to care either way. He walked toward her and took her in his arms. Molly gasped as he ran a hand down her spine, flattening her against him.

"What are you doing?"

He scored his thumb across her lip before continuing in a voice that melted her resistance, "Giving you that make-up kiss I owe you."

CHANCE WASN'T SURE that Molly was going to let him make love to her. At least not then. It was, after all, the middle of the workday.

Yet the moment he took her in his arms, he felt her cuddle against him. As if she had been waiting for and wanting this moment, too.

Grinning, he reached into his pocket. Found the little branch of leaves and berries he had been carrying around in his pocket. "I also want to get at least one kiss in under the mistletoe this holiday season," he teased, holding it above her head.

She rose up on tiptoe, the scent of her inundating his senses. "I think," she whispered, her yearning for him clear as day, "this is the place where I get a kiss in under the mistletoe, too." Her mouth opened beneath his, and their tongues mated in an erotic dance. Pleasure swept through him as he stepped between her legs. Anchoring an arm beneath her softly curving derriere, he lifted her up and situated her so her weight was against his middle. She wrapped her legs snugly around his waist, and his blood heated even more.

He carried her down the hall to his bedroom,

loving the way she felt against him, so warm and womanly. Their eyes locked as he set her down next to the bed. Undressing her felt extraordinarily intimate, pleasurable.

She eased off his shirt, kissing him, her lips softening beneath his. She clung to him, her fingers dipping into his shoulders, back and hips. Savoring everything about this moment, he delighted in the sweet taste of her. Of the way she continued undressing him, just as he had unwrapped her.

They drank in the sight of each other. She moaned as he rained kisses across her cheek, behind her ear, down the slope of her neck, before zeroing in on her mouth again.

She surged up against him, wrapping her arms around him, then tumbled him onto the bed.

He laughed in surprise. Tempestuous need glittered in her eyes as she followed him down and playfully straddled his middle. She threaded her fingers through his hair and stretched her body out languidly over the length of his, her heat cradling his pulsing hardness. He knew she thought this was just about sex. But it wasn't, he thought, as he let her deepen their kisses and rock against him. It was so much more.

Determined to make this lovemaking more memorable than either of them had ever had, he rolled so she was beneath him. He parted her knees and lay between her thighs. She came up off the bed as his lips lowered, suckling gently. Her thighs fell even farther apart as Chance kissed and stroked. And still it wasn't enough for either of them.

Molly teetered on the edge as he found a way to touch her that made her feel pleasure and desired, wanted and protected. Although she had promised herself she would wait for him, there was no delaying. She shuddered and fell apart in his arms. He held her tenderly until the aftershocks passed, then took her mouth again in a long, hot, tempestuous kiss. She shivered as the hardness of his chest teased the sensitive buds of her breasts, and lower still, the velvety hardness of his arousal nestled against her sex. She was so wet and so ready. And still he kissed her, until she throbbed and whimpered low in her throat. And only then, when she could stand it no longer, did he slide inside in one smooth, languid stroke. She clenched around him as he filled her completely. Taking her and making her his. Letting her possess him in response. Until her wildest Christmas wish was every dream fulfilled.

Afterward, Molly snuggled against him. He stroked a hand through her hair. Then she asked, "Would you ever consider moving to Dallas?"

His hand stilled. He continued to study her as if trying to figure something out. "I grew up there, Molly."

She focused on the unmistakable warning in his voice. "And never want to go back?"

His eyes darkened. "I don't mind visiting."

You'll never get what you want if you don't try. She drew on all the courage she possessed. "Would you ever consider visiting Braden and me, when we move there next month?"

He sat up against the headboard, the sheet draped low across his hips. "As…?"

Molly drew her gaze away from the flat plane of his abdomen. A distracting shiver tore through her. "What we are now. Friends."

He ran a hand down her arm. "Lovers?"

She wished he didn't look so damn good, even in his disheveled state. "If we can work it out." It would mean babysitters. Rendezvousing. Arranging things in a way that wouldn't leave Braden—or her—confused.

Molly understood that Chance wanted more than that.Yet he also had to know what a big step this was for her.

He watched her tug the sheet a little more snugly beneath her arms. "Does this mean we're exclusive?"

Heat gathered in her chest, and spread, from the tops of her breasts into her face. She worried her bottom teeth with her lip. "Does it?"

"I already feel that way about you, darlin'."

Molly relaxed. Her body nestled against his.

"I don't want you seeing anyone else, either," she admitted softly.

"Then that settles it." He pulled her against him for a long, thorough kiss that quickly had her tingling from head to toe. "We're officially a couple."

She splayed a hand over his broad chest, aware they still had a few hurdles left. "We will be," she stipulated firmly. "After the Open House your mother is hosting."

He paused. "What are you talking about?"

Molly swallowed and sat up against the headboard. She had to be completely honest with him or this would never work. "Lucille has invited me to attend as her protégé. She wants to give my design business a big boost."

"I knew that."

She wet her lips. "If it were known that I was also seeing you romantically, it might look like I was only with you to get ahead, or she was just helping me as a favor to you."

He sobered understandingly. "You'd be called a gold digger."

She nodded. Embarrassed, but determined. "I don't want to complicate my business future like that." She jerked in a breath, rushed on. "Because if Braden does get accepted at Worthington Academy, I'm really going to need more than just the two small jobs I already have lined up to make a real go of it."

She studied him, a wry smile tugging at the corners of her lips. "So, can you keep our relationship under the covers for just a little while longer?"

It was Chance's turn to look pained. "Are we talking weeks?"

"I'd rather not say anything until much later in the spring."

So months, he realized unhappily. He pushed a little higher against the headboard, too. "You don't think people are going to catch on to us spending so much time together?"

Molly took his hand. "If I were still living

in Laramie, yes, of course. If I'm in Dallas… it's a lot easier to keep things on the down low there if we stay out of the high-profile places." She squeezed his hand lightly. "What are you thinking?"

Chance frowned. "I've never been asked to stay in the shadows before. Usually people are all too eager to claim a relationship with me, whether one really exists or not."

"Exactly." Molly laid her head on his shoulder. "You're the son of Lucille and Frank Lockhart. You come from one of the most socially prominent families in the state. People want to make use of that connection." She lifted his hand to her lips, kissed the back of it.

"Only you don't," he said, threading his fingers through her hair, lifting her face to his. He slanted his mouth over hers, kissed her again, softly, appreciatively.

Her worry, that they wouldn't be able to make this work long-term, fading, Molly swung her body lithely over top of his. Her heart swelling with all she felt for him, she confided, "I don't want anything from you. Except friendship." She nipped playfully at his lips. "And this…" To show him how deeply she cared, she made love with him all over again.

Chapter Ten

"What you got me, Cowboy Chance?" Braden asked early one evening, a week and a half later when Chance came through the door, another yuletide shopping bag in hand.

"Whoa now. You don't know that's for you," Molly told her son. Although for most of the last ten nights, Chance had been there with her and her little boy, baking cookies, and working on their Christmas village in progress.

But prior to this, he had shown up with only one new item at a time.

Molly had appreciated his restraint.

Tonight, however, appeared to be different, Molly noticed as she and Chance exchanged looks.

"That's true." Chance backed up her efforts to instill manners in her little boy. He hung his jacket up and walked over to the sofa. "But as it happens—" he winked at Braden as they drew all three folding chairs up to the folding tables "—what's in here is for you and your mommy."

"Can I see?" Braden asked eagerly. "Please?"

Chance motioned for Molly to sit down on the other side of her son. He opened up the bag and lifted out a rectangular figurine. "Let's start with this."

Braden's eyes widened in appreciation. "That looks like our house," Molly said of the bungalow with the white picket fence.

Her son set them up carefully between the ranch and the North Pole.

Chance opened the bag. Braden pulled out

more. "Mrs. Santa Claus!" her son exclaimed. "And more reindeer!"

"To go with Rudolph and the sleigh."

Braden hopped up and down and put them in the North Pole section of their Christmas village.

"Maybe we should let Mommy open the next one," Chance said.

Braden clapped. "Yes. Mommy do it!"

Not sure what this was all about since Chance wouldn't tell her much except that he had decided he needed to vastly accelerate his "plan," to allow for more focus on the Leo and Lizzie train set as they got closer to Christmas, Molly opened it up. Inside were two figurines to add to the ones Chance had already brought. One of a modern Western woman with auburn hair similar to Molly's, and one of a redheaded little boy—also in Western gear. Beneath the figurines, Chance had written the identifying information.

"Gosh," he said, leading the conversation.

"That sure looks like you, Mommy. And this one looks like you, Braden."

"I think it is us!" Touched, Molly laid her hand across her heart.

Braden admired both, then reverently put them by the bungalow with the white picket fence. He studied the scene for a long, thoughtful moment.

To Molly and Chance's mutual dismay, his happiness turned to confusion. Plaintively, he walked over to Chance and looped his arms around their visitor's neck. "Where you, Cowboy Chance?"

"SORRY ABOUT THAT," Molly said after Braden had finally gone to sleep. She moved around the kitchen, baking that evening's batch of cookies—*hausfreunde*. "When Braden gets stuck on a question, sometimes he can't get off of it."

Chance understood the little boy's need to make them a family. He felt it, too. He sampled the buttery almond-apricot sandwich cookie dipped in bittersweet chocolate that Molly handed him. "Do you want me to get a likeness of myself?"

Molly dipped another cookie, then set it on waxed paper to dry. "I don't know. I mean... you might not even be with us next year." She paused to send him a hesitant glance—the kind that only came up when they were discussing their relationship.

She swallowed, her soft lips compressing, and turned her glance away. "If the long-distance thing doesn't work..."

He caught her around the waist and tugged her close. Bending his head, he kissed her lips lightly. Tasting chocolate. "It'll work, Molly. And I'll be here."

He studied her as they drew apart. "So what else is going on?"

Molly bent her head over her baking, a clear sign she was evading. "What do you mean?"

He gave her the room she seemed to need. "I could tell something was bothering you the minute I walked in the door."

This time, Molly did look up. Her eyes glittered with disappointment. "I received a letter in the mail today. Braden was wait-listed at Worthington Academy."

Chance didn't know whether to celebrate the fact that Molly's reasons for leaving Laramie in January had just diminished or share in her deep disappointment. "I'm sorry, darlin'." He took a seat on the other side of the island. *Tread cautiously.* "Did they say why?"

"No." Molly's lips twisted into a troubled line. "But I was offered a Skype conference with the headmistress and admissions counselor, so I plan to see what kept him from getting in, and what his chances are of getting off the wait list. And if they aren't good, if there is a chance he will be admitted in the fall semester."

Chance couldn't help but be disappointed that Molly had yet to change her mind about enrolling Braden there. He sent her a brief commiserating glance. Then, speaking from his own heart, he encouraged firmly, "Braden's a great kid, Molly. He will thrive no matter where he is."

"I know." Her eyes still glimmered with tears, but she shook off the rising emotion. "I just really wanted him to have this opportunity. But if he doesn't get it this year, I've already got a deposit down at a safety preschool in the area where I intend to rent a house."

Now it was Chance who felt like he'd received a major blow. Not that he hadn't been warned. He had. "Have you put a deposit down on a home, too?" He kept his attitude casual.

"No." Molly relaxed, as well. "That's the good thing about Dallas. It's so big there are plenty of places that would fit my needs in the short term."

If he couldn't dissuade her, he could sure as hell join her.

"You'll let me know if there is anything I can do to help?"

She smiled at him sweetly. "Of course. But I think I've got everything covered…

Meaning what? Chance wondered.

She didn't need him?

Or didn't want to need him?

How was he going to change that? He wondered, perplexed. Because he sure as hell was beginning to need them.

"IS THERE SOMETHING WRONG?" Molly asked Lucille several long, productive days later, when she arrived at the site to find her client upset.

She exchanged puzzled looks with Chance. He seemed as out of the loop as she felt.

"Is there something you don't like, Mom?" he asked in a low tone.

Heaven knew they didn't want Chance's mother to be unhappy with the renovation. This was their first joint project. The reputation of both their contracting firms was at stake.

Lucille glanced around at the finished backsplash, gleaming new appliances, countertops. Although the tile was newly sealed, there were smudges on the windows and stickers on the appliances. The newly finished wood floors bore the occasional dusty footprint. But all that was to be expected.

"We'll get a cleaning crew in here as soon as the touch-up painting is finished. The whole house will sparkle before we bring a speck of furniture in next week."

Lucille waved off the concern. "The renovation looks even better than I imagined. It's the Open House."

Sage walked in. Chance's eldest brother, Garrett, and his wife, Hope—a crisis manager and public relations expert—were at her side. "We got your message," Garrett said, cradling their nine-month-old son, Max, in his arms. The former army doc was now Lockhart Foundation CEO and medical director of West Texas Warrior Assistance.

Hope kissed her mother-in-law's cheek. "I'm not sure we understand the message you left."

Lucille fretted, "You all know I sent out a ton of invitations."

"Because you want to raise as much money as possible for the military vets we're helping," Garrett said.

"Most of the people I invited live in Dallas or Fort Worth. Since it's the holidays, I didn't think we would have that many acceptances."

"Let me guess," Sage said. "You were pleasantly surprised."

Lucille threw up her hands in distress. "We have four *hundred* people coming—so far. I don't know where we're going to put everyone!"

Hope already had her phone out. "It's not a problem. I can get some tents and tables and chairs. Heaters, too, if that cold front continues our way."

"I'll just make a lot more food," Sage said, with a former caterer's aplomb.

Lucille paced. "We're talking five days from now."

"It will work out, Mom." Chance wrapped his arm around Lucille's shoulders.

"The ranch house will not just be done—it

will be letter perfect," Molly promised. "It will be decorated beautifully inside and out, too."

Lucille frowned. "What about entertainment? If it was a much smaller gathering, I was just going to have holiday music playing unobtrusively in the house, but now..."

"Some of the military vets have a band," Garrett said, shifting his son a little higher in his arms. "They've played at some of our parties."

"They're really good," Hope put in. She grinned as Max reached over and tangled his fingers in her hair. Pulling her close, he gave his mommy a kiss.

Molly envied the sight of Garrett, Hope and Max. They made such a cute little family. The kind she could have if only she stayed.

"I'll see if I can get the band to play," Garrett offered.

The meeting went on for another twenty minutes. Finally, everyone left. Molly walked out with Chance to get the lights and garlands that she planned to go ahead and string on the front porch. She sent him a companionable glance. Strange as it was, just now she'd felt a little like family. Maybe because the Lockharts had gone out of their way to include her.

"I've never seen your mom that rattled."

Frowning, Chance carried the stepladder onto the porch. "It's because she hasn't seen a lot of those folks since she left Dallas."

Molly took the lights out of the packaging. "Sage said some of them had turned their backs on Lucille when the scandal regarding the Lockhart Foundation came to light."

The brackets on either side of Chance's mouth deepened. "Actually," he reported grimly, snapping his tool belt around his waist, "it was most of the people Mom knew."

"That must have been hard."

Chance propped the ladder against the roof of the porch and began to climb. "The amazing thing is Mom doesn't blame them. She says if she had been guilty of withholding funds from the nonprofits the foundation claimed it was helping, they'd be right to dismiss her. Anyway, she's all about the fresh start, concentrating on what really matters."

Molly handed him the end of the strand. "And for her, that's helping people."

He secured it to the newly painted facing. "And taking care of her family." Having put up as much as he could reach from that vantage point, he climbed back down the ladder.

Molly tilted her face to his. "What's important to you?"

He grabbed her around the waist, tugging her close. "Right now?" He waggled his brows teasingly. "You."

Before she could stop him, he had delivered a slow, deep kiss that had her knees ready to buckle, her toes tingling.

Molly planted her hands on the center of his chest. "Chance," she reprimanded. "Someone might see."

The pleasure they'd experienced faded. His expression became inscrutable once again.

"Right." He nodded, compliant but clearly un-happy, too. "We're still on the down low…"

Molly swallowed. She didn't want to hurt him, but she had to be honest about her needs. "It's just until I get my business efforts in Dallas off the ground," she said.

Chance stepped back, something even more indecipherable in his hazel eyes. "Does that mean I'm uninvited to the preschool program this evening?"

"No. Braden really wants you there. But I think it might be better if we drove separately, and then met up at my house later for a little after-school program gala for Braden." She paused. "Does that sound okay?"

A muscle ticked in his jaw. And for a mo-ment, Molly thought he was going to say, *No, it isn't okay at all*. Then the moment passed. He climbed right back up the ladder again. She handed him the next section of the light strand. "What time should I be there?" Chance asked quietly.

Molly relaxed. "The program starts at seven," she informed him with a relieved smile. "I'll save you a seat." It was going to make Braden so happy, having Chance there. Her, too.

"CHANCE LOCKHART, WHAT are you doing at a preschool program?" Mary Beth Simmons, the local PTA president and resident busybody, demanded.

Practicing my down low, Chance thought grumpily, then shrugged and mimed total innocence. "I heard it was an event not to be missed."

Mary Beth squinted. "Who told you that?"

First rule of hiding something? Not that he'd had a lot of experience. *Be as honest as possible.* "Braden Griffith," he said and watched Mary Beth's gaze turned speculative. "Molly Griffith and I combined forces on a rush job for my mom, so we've been seeing a lot of each other. I've gotten to know her son. Cute kid."

Mary Beth tilted her head. "There are a lot of cute kids in Laramie, Chance."

True enough. He flashed an indulgent smile. "Most of them have a ton of family. Braden doesn't." He leaned toward her in a gossipy manner, meant to satisfy her need to be in the know. "And I think, times like this, the little tyke is beginning to notice the difference between his life, and—" Chance nodded at little Ava Monroe, who had her own fan club of McCabes and Monroes in attendance.

Chastened, Mary Beth straightened. "I see what you mean."

"Anyway, since I was invited, I volunteered to make his lack of extended cheerleaders not so obvious for little Braden."

Mary Beth laid a hand across her heart. "What a giving thing for you to do," she said, impressed.

Chance flashed a humble grin. "'Tis the season…"

"What was that about?" Molly asked, discreetly texting him as soon as he sat down next to her.

Aware she smelled like orchids…which meant she was wearing that perfume he liked. And that this was the closest thing to a date—albeit a clandestine one—that they'd ever had, Chance pulled out his phone and texted her back. I was pretending I was dragged here as a Good Samaritan.

"Oh." Molly formed the words with her soft lips.

He leaned down and whispered in her ear, longing for the day when they would have actual dates. And more. "We both know that's not the case." He hadn't been dragged. He'd been elated to be invited.

Around them, other phones and video cameras were being readied. He lifted a curious brow. Molly explained. "Everyone's going to record it."

"How about I record, and you just watch? I'll email it to you later. That way you can just enjoy."

"Thank you."

He stifled a smile and kept looking straight ahead at the stage. "My pleasure."

They stopped talking at that point. Nevertheless, they got a lot of curious looks despite their efforts to be casual. Soon the kids marched up onstage, proud as could be, and the program started.

Chance was glad he was focused on recording. Otherwise someone might have seen the tear that came to his eyes as Braden puffed out his little chest, and belted out "We Wish You a Merry Christmas" and a half-dozen other holiday tunes at the top of his little lungs. That was, when Braden wasn't grinning and waving at Molly and him.

When the program came to an end, Chance was on his feet, clapping and whistling and hooting, as proud as any parent there. Everyone else was so caught up in the proud moment that his enthusiasm went unnoticed.

By all but Molly—and Braden.

"Cowboy Chance!" Braden cried, hustling

down from the stage. "Hey, everybody!" He turned and waved vigorously at his two frequently mentioned best friends. "Come see—Cowboy Chance!"

Will and Justin got permission from their parents and hightailed it to Braden's side. "He's got bulls!" Braden declared loudly.

Molly realized her son's vowel sounded more like an *a* than a *u*.

Several horrified adults turned in their direction.

"Black Angus bucking bulls of the national championship variety," Molly explained cheerfully to one and all.

A few parents, apparently not familiar with rodeo terms, looked even more confused.

"And barns!" Braden yelled blithely, as everyone around them chuckled at his earlier mispronunciation.

"And lots of other things, as well," Chance added. "Like bull barns."

"And fences!" Braden shouted.

"And training facilities."

"And *baby* bulls!" Braden repeated his earlier mispronunciation while slinging an index finger in Chance's direction. A gesture that, thanks to the discrepancy in their heights, ended up pointing a foot below Chance's waist.

More chuckles.

A few of the guys sent sympathetic, dad-to-dad glances Chance's way.

Which would have been funny, Chance thought, as the merry double entendres flying right above the toddler's heads increased, if not for Molly's increased embarrassment. Determined to spare them all any more unnecessary attention from the crowd, Chance knelt down so he and the little boy he adored were at eye level. He put his hand on Braden's shoulder. "Proud of you, buddy," he said fiercely, meaning it with all his heart. "That was a *great* job, singing."

Chance expected Braden to grin the way he always did when he was praised. He didn't expect him to look at Chance with equal affection and lift his hands, wordlessly asking to be picked up the way a lot of the other three-year-olds were being picked up for hugs by their dads.

A lump in his throat, Chance complied.

Braden hooked his hands around Chance's neck and hugged him like he never wanted to let go. For the first time in his life, Chance had an inkling, a real inkling of what it would be like to be a father. And not just any father. Braden's daddy.

He liked it.

Almost as much as he liked the idea of one day being Molly's husband. Wasn't that a Christmas surprise?

Chapter Eleven

"There is no doubt Braden is a very bright little boy," Worthington Academy's psychologist, Dr. Mitchard, said when the Skype conference Molly had requested began. "He had no trouble conversing on any subject that interested him. Like bulls."

Oh, dear.

"And Cowboy Chance."

Somehow Molly managed to keep a poker face. Even as her heart skipped a beat just hearing Chance's name.

"However, when we attempted to get him to focus on the word or number problems presented to him, he refused to speak," the headmistress told Molly.

"At all?" Molly could hardly believe it. Yes, her son's sentences were rudimentary, but Braden always had something to say. In fact, the hardest thing to do was get him to stop talking.

The psychologist, who had supervised the testing, nodded. "Even when he seemed to know the answer to our inquiries, which I'm sorry to relate, wasn't all that often, he refused to divulge it to us."

"Additionally, he does not have the background of second language, early reading and math, music and art instruction that our accepted students have. Hence, it's our considered opinion that he's not ready for such a rigorous academic pre-K curriculum," Elspeth Pyle said.

"If you know all that," Molly said, feeling hurt and confused, "why did you invite us to come all the way to Dallas for an in-depth admissions interview?" *Why did you have me drop every-thing to be there on such short notice?*

The two women exchanged glances.

The headmistress said, "Because we are al-ways looking to diversify as much as we can, without lowering our high standards, and we don't currently have anyone in the three-year-old class who has come from a rural environment."

"Actually," Molly said, recognizing an evasion when she heard one, "we live in town."

"Well, he talked like he spent an inordinate time on a bull ranch!" the psychologist said.

"We were confused as to whether he might be living there, instead of the address on the appli-cation," Elspeth Pyle reiterated.

Chagrined, Molly admitted, "No. We've never stayed there." *Much as I might have wished.* "Braden's just visited a few times. He loves all animals, though." She spun it as best she could. "And he'd never seen any kind of cattle opera-tion in person. So I guess it made a bigger im-pression on him than I realized."

"Perhaps so." The two administrators exchanged tense smiles. "Do you have any more questions?" Elspeth asked.

"Just one." Molly asked with a determined smile. "What are my son's chances of getting off the wait list?"

"At this point, not good. Not good at all."

"WHAT YOU GOT, Cowboy Chance?" Braden asked several hours later when Chance stopped by just before bedtime, gift bag in hand, and scooped him up in his strong arms.

"A Christmas cowboy?" Braden hoped. He wrapped his arms around Chance's neck, giving him a happy hug. "Just like you?"

"I think we might get a couple more people for the village," Molly said in an effort not to put Chance on the spot. Not that the rugged rancher seemed to mind the request. "They have them at Monroe's Western Wear in town."

Chance set Braden in the middle of the sofa and sat down on one side of him. Molly took the other, watching as Chance opened up the by-now-familiar gift bag. "Let's see." Chance pulled out the first rotund figurine.

"Santa!" Braden clapped his hands.

"And look." He plucked out three Black Angus cattle figures.

"Mommy, daddy and baby bull!" Braden shouted excitedly.

"Hmm." Molly played along with the thoughtful gambit as her son kissed his new figures and hugged them to his chest. "Looks like the toy Santa Claus brought you the toy bull family that you wanted."

"And—" Chance plucked out a small square of Astroturf, surrounded by fence "—a pasture for them to stay in."

Braden turned to her. He seemed to understand in the brief silence that fell that this was a very elaborate consolation prize. So much for the school officials who had deemed him not able to understand enough, Molly thought in vindication.

"Real...want real...for me," Braden said emphatically, looking frustrated they still didn't understand what he was trying to communicate.

Except they did, Molly thought wistfully, withholding a sigh.

Solemnly, Chance interjected, "I talked to Santa on the phone about that."

Oh, boy, they were in dangerous territory now. Territory they probably should have discussed beforehand. On the other hand, Braden was far more willing to accept what Chance said as gospel than anything his mere mother stated. Probably because Chance cut such a heroic figure. Which was definitely an anomaly around their house...

Braden stared, wide-eyed. "You call Santa?"

Chance shifted Braden onto his lap with the ease of a natural daddy. "He was very upset that he couldn't do this for you, because Santa Claus knows what a very good boy you have been this year, but he said a real bull family would not fit on his sleigh. He only has room to bring you a very special toy present. And you know what I said?"

Braden considered. Finally, he screwed up his little face into a hopeful expression.

"I said, that you know that all the toys that Santa brings are so very special, that you will be happy with whatever Santa brings you."

"WELL, DO YOU THINK we handled it?" Chance asked Molly after they tucked Braden into bed.

A sentimental look on her pretty face, Molly paused to admire the Christmas village they had put together over the course of the last weeks. It had a ranch like Chance's, a bull family, a house that looked like hers, figures that represented her and Braden, and a North Pole with Santa, sleigh and reindeer. The only thing it didn't have was Chance. As Braden had once again noted. The thing that sucked was that Chance wanted to be represented in the panorama that had come to mean so much to Braden, too.

What Molly wanted, however, was a lot more tenuous.

She wanted temporary. He wanted much more. But opinions could change. And he knew how to build on small successes, turn them into more.

"I think so." Molly turned and went into the kitchen, where she was preparing *Lebkuchen*. "I mean, you saw the way his face lit up at the Toy Emporium."

The tantalizing smell of fresh-baked German gingerbread cookies filled the space. Chance settled opposite her, predicting softly, "It'll be a big moment."

Molly bent to pipe white icing on each confection. "It will." She handed him a finished treat to taste. It was, as he had expected, completely delicious. As was everything she made.

Molly eyed him closely. A pulse was suddenly throbbing in her throat. "You know, you were such a big part of it, I think we should invite you. But—" she lifted a wary hand

"—only if you want to see him when he first lays eyes on it."

He circled the counter and took her in his arms, aware how frequent moments like these could be if they joined forces and lived not just in the same county but under the same roof. "Is that an invitation to stay the night?"

She relaxed into the curve of his body, looking deep into his eyes. "Ah, no. I'm not doing that until I get married. And who knows if that will ever be."

But she was talking about it. Mulling over the possibility. A month ago she wouldn't have even done that.

He smiled, willing to be patient a little while longer. "Then how will this work?"

She looked up at him, as if in awe how good it felt to simply hang out this way. "Um…well, we could set the time for your arrival on Christmas morning at 5:00 a.m." An affectionate twinkle lit her amber gaze. "If he's not awake yet, we could have *stollen* and coffee while we wait.

Then open presents and have a proper man-size breakfast later."

Her excitement was contagious. He kissed her temple. "It's a date."

Smiling, Molly went back to icing cookies.

Chance lounged against the counter. "By the way, how did the Skype meeting with the Worthington Academy staff go this afternoon?" He wanted to hear that Elspeth Pyle, Dr. Mitchard and the others had been as considerate of Molly's feelings as they would have been to any of the wealthy parents they dealt with.

Unfortunately, that did not appear to have been the case. Her expression troubled, Molly briefly related what had been said to her. He couldn't have disagreed more.

"They're wrong about Braden being ready for a more rigorous program," Chance said fiercely. "I've spent time with him. I know he could more than handle whatever they threw at him."

Molly grinned. "Watch it. You're sounding like a proud papa." As soon as the words were out, she blushed. Averting her glance, she amended hastily, "You know what I mean."

Chance curved a comforting hand around her shoulder. "I do," he admitted solemnly. "And you're right. I am very protective of him." *And you, too*, Chance added silently. *Much more than you know.*

Looking as if the Skype meeting had brought out all her worst insecurities, Molly nodded, admitting, "It's hard not to be protective with little kids. They're so vulnerable."

"True." Sensing she needed him more than she would admit, he turned to her and pulled her all the way into his arms. "But there's something very special about Braden." He stroked a gentle hand through her hair and lifted her face to his. "I felt a connection to him the first time we met."

"And he, you," Molly said, her shoulders tense in a way they hadn't been before they'd begun talking about Worthington Academy.

"Did they say anything else?" Chance pressed, wanting to know the whole story.

"No." Her casual, self-effacing tone hinted at the vulnerability she felt inside. "It was more a feeling I had."

He waited. Guilt that she might have found out what he had done to put her in this position, despite the precautions he had taken to prevent just such a revelation, roiled in his gut.

Molly shook her head, moving on to the next tray. "Like…" She struggled to put her intuition into words. "They'd been *forced* to interview him or something."

Maybe because they sort of had been.

He studied her, maintaining a poker face. "They said that?" His temper rose.

"No. It just…" She put more icing into the piping bag. "What they did say about needing to interview him for the diversity in backgrounds of their student body. I didn't buy it."

"How so?" he asked carefully.

"Well… I mean, you saw the children in the

classes we observed. Even in identical uniforms, you could see they were all privileged kids from wealthy backgrounds. Their haircuts, their perfect body mass indexes, their posture, their demeanor…" She sighed heavily. "These were all kids who were used to being pampered, revered, adored."

The same could easily be said about her son, except for coming from money. "Braden has confidence, too," he pointed out.

Molly's face took on the fierce, maternal line he knew so well. "Not the confidence that comes from never having to want for or worry about anything."

Money in the bank only went so far. Chance disagreed. "Confidence is confidence."

Molly huffed and went to the sink to rinse the icing off her fingers. "You say that because you come from the other side," she accused him over her shoulder. "The side that had all the advantages. I didn't."

Chance waited until she turned around, then

put a hand on either side of her, not touching her but effectively trapping her against the counter just the same. "Do you ever think that's part of what makes you who and what you are?"

His challenging tone had her lifting her chin. "And what am I?" she sassed.

Plenty. "Strong, independent, resilient, savvy, talented, gorgeous..." Watching the color come into her cheeks, he teased, "Shall I go on?"

She folded one arm against her waist, not touching him, either, and tapped her finger against her lips. "I like that you put my beauty at the end of the list." She wrinkled her nose playfully. "Such as it is."

Enough of her downgrading herself. He pulled her all the way into his arms, pressing her softness against his hardness. "What it is," he growled, "is amazing. Heart poundingly—" he paused to kiss her deeply "—wonderful."

She shook her head at him in silent remonstration. "You can stop now," she chided, even as her eyes filled with affection. "Compliments are not necessary."

Chance sobered. His heart ached for all that was still missing in her life. That could be so easily corrected. "They're not compliments, darlin'." He stroked his hand down her cheek and bent to kiss her again, tenderly this time. "They are heartfelt observations." And what he felt when he looked at her was all heart.

Chapter Twelve

"I can't believe we're doing this," Molly murmured the next afternoon. She stepped out of his shower and wrapped a towel around her.

Chance shut off the spigot, his body still humming from their last incredible bout of lovemaking. Blotting the dampness from his hair and skin, he hung up his towel and joined her at the mirror. Coming up behind her, he aligned his naked body against hers and planted a kiss on the back of her neck. "Taking a long lunch hour?"

Molly turned to give him a mischievous glance that swept over him hungrily from head to toe, then ran a brush through her hair, restoring order to her still-damp curls.

She pivoted to face him. As she pressed against him, he could feel how much she wanted him. If only they had the time…"I can't believe—" she sent him an alluring glance from beneath her lashes, her nipples pearling beneath the towel "—we're taking a long lunch hour in your bed."

"And shower," he teased, following her into the bedroom. "I can." His body humming with resurging need, he watched her bend to pick up her clothes. Not ready to see her leave just yet, he tugged her against him for a sweet, leisurely kiss. "I think that was the best pre-Christmas present I ever had."

"Me, too," Molly murmured, kissing him back even more languidly.

He threaded his hands through her hair, wishing he didn't have to worry about rushing her into the next step. "Besides—" he kissed his way down her throat "—with the Circle H ranch house finished…"

Molly flitted out of his arms with a reluctant sigh, then slipped on her satin burgundy panties and matching bra. Shifting into the business mode he knew so well, she reminded him, "We still have to help decorate the interior for the Open House at the Circle H tomorrow morning. Make sure Sage and her catering staff have everything they need for the evening's festivities."

Noting the pleat of new worry between her brows, he shifted into work gear, too. Pulling on his boxer briefs, then his jeans, he reassured her confidently. "It's all going to go smoothly. We have Garrett's wife, Hope, in charge, remember? There's no crisis my sister-in-law can't handle. So even if there are problems, and I'm not expecting any, Hope will find solutions for them."

"I know." Molly eased a black turtleneck sweater over her head.

Chance's mouth went dry as she shimmied

into her jeans. Dressed or undressed, she made him go hard with need. "Garrett and Wyatt have also volunteered to help. In fact, the only family member who won't be around to support Mom's entry back into the fund-raising nonprofit world will be Zane."

Molly sat down on the edge of his bed to tug on her favorite peacock-blue cowgirl boots. She extended one showgirl-quality leg, then the other. "Your mom mentioned Zane was going to try and get home for Christmas this year."

Chance nodded, his worry over his Special Forces brother briefly coming to the fore. "Even if he does make it, and there's no guarantee of that, it would likely be just in the nick of time, not for the Open House."

Molly sobered. "One of the disadvantages of serving in the military, I guess." Her frown deepened.

"I don't think Zane minds. In fact, I'm pretty sure he thrives on all the uncertainty and danger."

Molly nodded, her mood becoming even more distant.

Chance wrapped his hands around her waist and tugged her close. He bent his head to nuzzle the softness of her hair, inhale the sexy fragrance that was uniquely her. "My question is, what's really bugging you today?" Loving the way she felt in his arms, he kissed his way across her temple. She'd been moody all morning. Which was why he'd suggested their noontime rendezvous rather than try to get an actual date with her that evening. "The only time I've had your full attention is when we were making love."

She blushed in a way that made her look prettier, more womanly than ever, then admitted wryly, "Listen, cowboy, it's a little hard to think of anything else when you're...um..."

He chuckled, a deep rumbling low in his throat. "I know." He caressed the slender curve of her hip. "And don't think you're going to distract me asking me to show you what other ex-traordinary skills I have."

For a second, she looked just as tempted as he felt.

"Seriously." He brushed the pad of his thumb across her lower lip, wanting to help her out if he could. He looked deep into her eyes. "What's bothering you?"

Molly balled her hands into fists and blew out a frustrated breath. "If you must know, I don't have anything appropriate to wear to the Open House."

Chance squinted. "I've seen your closet, Molly. You're a clotheshorse."

She walked out of his bedroom and down the stairs, leaving him to follow. "Yes, but my clothes aren't designer duds. Which is why your lovely sister, Sage, volunteered to act as my stylist for the evening and lent me an absolutely gorgeous cocktail dress and the accessories that went with it."

He caught up with her in the kitchen. "That was nice of her."

Figuring she had to be as hungry as he was, he pulled out the cold cuts and cheeses. Handed her a plate and a loaf of multigrain bread.

With a sigh, she began assembling a sandwich. "Yes, well, we lamented our wardrobe crises together."

He got a plate and did the same. "What has Sage got to worry about?"

Molly looked in his fridge and brought out the mayo, spicy mustard and leaf lettuce. "Promise you won't mention it to her?"

Chance made an X over the center of his chest.

With a commiserating moue, Molly told him, "She had to have the dress she planned to wear to the gala let out at the seams. Apparently she's gained a little weight since coming back to Texas and opening her café bakery."

Chance shook his head in consternation. If he lived to be a hundred he would never understand why women worried about the shift of a few pounds in either direction.

He cut his sandwich in half, then went to find the chips. "Hard to see how, since she's had the stomach flu twice in the past six weeks."

Molly took a seat beside him at the island. "I heard she had been under the weather a couple of times." She picked up a sandwich that was as thin as his was thick. "Anyway, I have to get over there in forty-five minutes to pick up the dress, so as soon as I finish this, I've got to run."

He poured a couple of glasses of iced tea, not about to let her go before he'd nailed down their next time together. "Will I see you tonight?"

If she was free, maybe he could talk her into an official date. Even if they had to go all the way to San Angelo to have it, to avoid her fear of being seen together socially.

"Tomorrow morning. I have to spend the evening completing the pre-enrollment paperwork for Braden's new preschool in Dallas. They need it before Christmas if he's going to start there in January."

Chance was happy Molly had selected a place other than the high-stress Worthington Academy to put her son. Not so happy it was a good 150 miles away. He forced himself to be supportive anyway. "How does he feel about the move?" Chance asked cheerfully.

Molly broke a potato chip in two. "I haven't told him."

Chance narrowed his gaze. Molly was usually very up front with her son about what was going to happen next. And what was expected of him.

Her cheeks turning pink, she explained, "Once I have a rental home picked out to go see and the school set up, we'll take another trip there. I'll explain it all then, when I can show him where we are going to live and so on."

Disappointment knotted his gut. "So you're really doing this?"

She wasn't surprised he didn't want to see her

go. However, his feelings did not change her mind. "I really am," she confirmed.

EXCEPT, MOLLY KNEW, as she left Chance and drove away from Bullhaven, she wasn't nearly as brave as she sounded.

The truth was the closer she got to actually making the big change, the more she did not really want to do it after all.

Yet the more rational part of her knew that she couldn't let last-minute jitters affect putting what had been a years-long plan for her and Braden's future into action.

Her son deserved the very best. She wanted him to have everything he could possibly have. The kind of opportunity and vast choices she had never been afforded.

She wanted the kind of financial security Chance and his siblings had grown up with, so that if, heaven forbid, anything ever happened to her, or Braden, she would have the money and resources to deal with it.

Right now she didn't.

And wouldn't if she stayed in the moderate-income range she currently enjoyed.

So like it or not, she was headed to the big city come January.

And she and Chance would have a casual, long-distance romance, or perhaps just fade out entirely.

Either way, she had to be a grown-up about it. She couldn't do what she did before with Aaron and be ready to base her whole life, all her plans for the future, on a man.

Because if her growing relationship with Chance didn't work out—as the affair with Braden's daddy hadn't—she would be devastated. Professionally and personally. The setbacks and fallout might be impossible to overcome.

She couldn't do that to herself. She couldn't do it to her son. So she would enjoy this Christmas the way she had never enjoyed a holiday before, she reassured herself fiercely, and move on from there.

"Sure you don't want me to pick you up?" Chance asked the following evening. Why was just the sound of his deep, gravelly voice so sexy? Why was his rock-solid presence so comforting and enticing? A lump rose to her throat as unbidden tears sprang to her eyes. Shaking off the unwelcome emotion, Molly finished slipping on the shoes that matched her borrowed dress.

Feeling part imposter, part Cinderella, she cradled the phone to her ear. "No, I have to drop off Braden. He's having a sleepover with Will and Justin tonight, at Justin's house."

"Ah." Chance chuckled softly. "Can we have a sleepover, too?"

Why not? Given how precious little time they had left to spend with each other. Plus, if the evening went as well as Lucille had predicted it would go for Molly, she'd likely have a lot to celebrate.

"Possibly," she murmured coyly, moving a small distance away from her son, who was busy playing with his Christmas village. "If you're a good boy and we're discreet."

"Oh, that can certainly be arranged, darlin'," he reassured her playfully. "So." His husky baritone was rife with promises. "My place?"

"Yes." She could leave very early tomorrow morning, before his hired hands arrived to take care of the bulls.

"See you soon then." His enthusiasm engendered her own. "And, Molly?"

Heavens, she was going to miss this man. So much. "Yes?"

"I want you to know." The warmth of his emotions kindled hers. "You and Braden have made this the best yuletide season of my life."

Molly smiled, knowing deep down she could not want for more. "Right back at you, cowboy."

SEVERAL HOURS LATER, Chance stood at the fringes of the crowd milling through the Open

House at the newly renovated Circle H ranch house, making good on his promise not to be seen with Molly. It wasn't easy keeping his distance. She looked gorgeous as hell in a shimmering emerald-green cocktail dress, black velvet evening blazer and stiletto heels.

As previously arranged, his mother had her arm looped through Molly's and was taking her around, introducing her as the hottest up-and-coming interior designer.

From what he could see, a lot of interest was being generated. Which meant Molly would soon be as successful and financially secure as she dreamed of being.

In Dallas…

While he was here. Right where he wanted to be. Or had, until she and her young son had sauntered into his life.

"A million bucks for your thoughts," Chance's younger brother Wyatt gibed, joining him.

They clinked glasses. "Very funny." Chance sipped his Bourbon & Branch.

"Actually, it's appropriate."

Chance lifted a brow at the most cynical of his siblings.

With a knowing smirk, Wyatt informed him, "Mr. X is here, with Babs and Delia, and they're coming for you."

Chance promptly changed the subject to something his horse-ranching brother would *not* want to discuss. "As long as we're talking about affairs that are long over," he said smugly, "I saw Adelaide Smythe." She was Wyatt's very single, very pregnant with twins ex-girlfriend from way back, who Wyatt had never really gotten over.

Wyatt remained unflappable. Which meant, Chance intuited, the two had already crossed swords.

"As the new CFO of Lockhart Foundation, Adelaide would be expected to be here. The piranhas on the lookout for you, however, would not."

So true, he admitted reluctantly. "Mom invited them?"

"Apparently, Garrett and Hope found out that

Mr. X has a reputation for supporting nonprofits geared to helping our military and their families, so they suggested to Mom that she invite the very deep-pocketed Mr. X. I don't think they expected him to show up personally. But then, they hadn't heard about how he'd been attempting to buy you out." Wyatt lifted his glass to Chance. He nodded toward the trio emerging from one of the tents. "And here they come..."

Wyatt stepped aside to make room, but he stayed to watch the show. The woman who would have been his mother-in-law closed in. "Last opportunity," Babs told Chance.

Mr. X looked at Chance, too. "I'll even go down to only a forty-nine percent stake in the business, if that will turn the tide in my favor."

Chance shook his head.

Delia rolled her eyes. "Chance is. Just. Not. Interested."

Babs sent an irritated look at her daughter. "Chance doesn't need you to defend him, sweetheart."

Wordlessly, Delia spun away and headed into the crowd. Mr. X followed.

Babs glared at Chance. "I'm going to get Delia to forget you once and for all, if it is the last thing I do, Chance Lockhart!"

Chance was pretty sure that was already the case. He relaxed as Babs stormed off.

"Is Delia still carrying a torch for you?" Wyatt asked curiously.

Chance shook his head. "No."

But Mr. X sure seemed to be intent on pursuing Delia. The slightly geeky billionaire caught up with Babs's daughter at the fringes and put his hand on her waist. Leaning down, he said something into her ear. Delia shrugged free. Took off. Mr. X was right behind her, looking more determined than ever.

Thirty seconds later, Chance got a text from Delia.

MOLLY SAW CHANCE winding through the crowd, walking past the bandstand toward the barns.

She was about to follow him, hoping to surreptitiously get a moment alone with him, when Babs stepped out in front of her.

For once, the aggressive sales and acquisitions exec was not with her daughter or Mr. X, who, to Molly's surprise, had both also appeared there that evening. "Hello, dear," Babs said cheerfully. "I'd like to speak to you about doing a decorating job for me."

Molly was not at the point she could turn down any business in her new city. Though if she could have, this would have been the job she passed on. Determined to be professional, she plucked her phone from her blazer pocket and brought up her calendar. "Absolutely."

Babs wrote the address on the back of her business card. "The job is here in Laramie County. A house on the lake that I'm considering buying as rental property. Can you be there at 9:00 a.m.? The Realtor is going to open up the house. Then we can talk about what is possible in terms of renovation."

Out of the corner of her eye, Molly saw Mr. X come out from behind the barn. He was alone, and he looked ticked off.

Wondering what that was about, Molly turned her attention back to Babs. "I'll see you then."

Babs pivoted to see what Molly had been looking at, then headed off in the direction of Mr. X. Molly continued threading her way through the dwindling crowds, toward the barn.

As she neared it, she saw Delia standing in the shadows just behind it, arms folded in front of her. Chance was standing opposite his ex. They were talking. Seriously, it seemed. Delia did not seem to like what she was hearing from her ex. She threw up her arms in frustration and walked away, head bowed.

What was going on here? Molly wondered, stalled in her tracks.

Was there still something left between Chance and Delia?

Had Mr. X discovered the two of them together? Or had the three of them been talking in private—about the bucking-bull business yet again?

She had no more chance to ponder because Chance was striding toward her. He stopped just short of her. He waited until they were well out of earshot of other partygoers passing by, then grinned casually and quipped, "Am I allowed to talk to you yet?"

"Yes," Molly said, ready to bolt this fundraiser once and for all. Right or wrong, she wanted the safety of Chance's arms. "Just not here," she said.

Chapter Thirteen

As soon as they got back to Bullhaven, Molly filled Chance in on her conversation with Delia's mother. Chance didn't even have to think about what his recommendation would be. "Turn her down," he said.

Molly slipped off her heels. Her lips slid out in the adorable pout he knew so well. And could never stop wanting to kiss. "I can't."

He lit the fire, then went into the kitchen and brought them back a couple of bottles of water. Molly sank onto his big leather sofa and bent over to rub her arches. "Babs is not just one of your mother's longtime friends—"

"I'm not sure I'd call them that exactly," Chance interrupted. "They're more like acquaintances who once frequented the same social scene."

Practically trembling with the exhaustion and adrenaline accumulated after such a long evening, Molly waved off his pointed objection. "Regardless, Babs is very well connected. Doing a job for her, and doing it well, could bring me a lot of future business."

Already wanting her so bad he ached, Chance shifted Molly into the corner of the leather sofa and drew her legs across his lap. Adjusting his posture to ease the pressure building at the front of his slacks, he massaged her left foot gently, from toes to heel. Felt her start to blissfully relax, even as his desire built. "She could also blackball you," he pointed out quietly.

Molly drew her legs away from his lap and swung them back onto the floor. Sitting up, she looked him straight in the eye. Beneath their evening clothes, their thighs touched. "Believe me, I am very well aware of that, too," she snapped. "That's why I'm treading carefully."

Yes, but you shouldn't have to, he thought, as a tense silence fell.

They stared at each other.

She sighed and ran her hands through her hair.

Finally, he tried again. "I talked to Delia tonight."

Molly's lips tightened. Briefly she turned her glance away, clearly angry now. "I know. I saw the two of you come out from behind the barn."

That sounded a lot worse than it had been. Knowing how lame it sounded, he explained, "She wanted to talk to me without her mother seeing."

Molly's delicate brow lifted, and the pink in her cheeks deepened. She folded her arms in front of her and glared at him. "Sounds cozy."

She wanted to believe him. He could see that. She just wasn't sure she should.

He tore his eyes from the lush fullness of her lips. "Delia's worried her mother and Mr. X are up to something."

Her expressive brows lowered over her long-lashed eyes. Molly uncapped her water bottle and took a long, thirsty drink. "That's hardly old news." She shrugged. "The two of them have been scheming ways to somehow buy out or takeover your bucking-bull business for weeks now."

"Something besides that," Chance clarified with concern.

"Like what?" Molly asked impatiently.

"Delia doesn't know. But Bab's sudden interest in hiring you indicates you're involved in her devious plans, too."

Molly flinched. He'd never seen her so overwrought or incredibly, passionately beautiful, and he edged closer.

"Babs couldn't just want me on board because I'm talented?"

Chance saw he'd hurt her feelings. But there

was too much at stake—most importantly, their relationship—to sugarcoat the situation. "No."

Molly's lips tightened. Slowly but surely the walls around her heart began to go back up. "Thanks a lot."

Wanting to protect her more than ever, he covered her hand with his. "Listen to me, Molly. Mr. X told Delia he's prepared to pull out all the stops to get her to go out with him. And Babs is a manipulative shrew who never forgets a slight."

"So?" Molly shook her head as if that would clear it. "How is any of that our problem?"

"Babs blames me for the fact her only daughter has never married or brought a new influx of major money into their family coffers. She's particularly unhappy about the fact that Delia has been rejecting all of Mr. X's advances thus far. And she's told Delia repeatedly that she would like nothing better than to see me as unhappy as Delia has been. Worse, Babs apparently realized correctly the best way to get her long-awaited revenge on me is through you, Molly." Chance paused to let his words sink in. "I don't want you getting hurt via collateral damage," Chance finished tersely. *I don't want Babs ruining what we have.*

And it was so fragile, Babs just might.

Molly huffed out a breath. "I think you're overreacting."

Chance only wished he was.

Extricating her hand from his, she stood and moved gracefully to the fireplace. She stood with her back to the flames. "Babs doesn't know we're dating. Nor does anyone else. Everyone thinks we've just buried the hatchet long enough to become temporary co-contractors on your mother's renovation and casual friends."

Chance wasn't so sure about that. Molly wore her heart on her sleeve, whether she realized it or not.

He was equally bad at hiding his feelings where she was concerned. Whether she liked it or not, the two of them had been getting a lot of curious looks. People, like his siblings and their crews, were starting to put two and two together. Heck, even three-year-old Braden realized they'd forged a heck of a lot more than a casual connection. And could have a lot more, if Molly would only give them a shot.

Unwilling to see what was right in front of her, Molly continued blithely, defiantly keeping her blinders on. "So there's no reason for Babs to come after me."

Okay. So Molly didn't want to believe him. Maybe because she had yet to see the dark side of the world he had grown up in. She'd been raised in Laramie County, where neighbor took care of neighbor, and a man or woman's word was worth more than any gold.

He would have to accept her naive outlook in this matter, and for now, at least, try another tact. "Why risk it, in any case?" he said with a reassuring smile. He rose and joined her at the hearth. "There will be other jobs."

"It doesn't matter if there are, or aren't."

Molly angled her chin at him, fury glittering in her amber eyes. "I'm not like you, Chance. I don't have the luxury of turning down work or money!" Her slender body quivered with emotion. "I can't just throw lucrative offers into the shredder without even looking at them."

He returned her pointed look. "You did it once—with Braden's daddy."

"Yes." Sadness turned the corners of her mouth down. "And I've regretted it ever since."

MOLLY DIDN'T KNOW where the words had come from. She could barely fathom thinking them, never mind saying them aloud. To Chance, of all people.

He clasped her elbow lightly and drew her toward him. "You don't mean that," he said quietly.

The truth hit her with the force of the north wind, chilling her from head to toe. Ignoring the shocked and disillusioned expression on Chance's face, she lifted her face to his and went on with gut-wrenching clarity. "I'm not saying it would have been the right thing to do." She knew, deep down, that morally and ethically it would not have been.

Chance's wish to understand her helped her go on. "Given how Braden's daddy felt about having a child at all, never mind with me, it would have been disastrous to bring Aaron into the equation. Because all Braden would have been to Aaron was a problem to be managed." Her voice cracked a little. "And Braden would have been devastated to realize he wasn't loved or wanted the way he should be."

Chance twined his hands with hers. Squeezed. "I agree."

Molly was determined to let Chance see the differences between them as clearly as she did. She looked him in the eye. "But that doesn't mean I don't wish—on some level, anyway—that I could have figured out a way back then to provide for and protect Braden. Even if it injured my pride."

She paused to let her words sink in.

"Because if I had accepted the money to just go away, then I would be able to afford to put Braden in any elite school I chose without asking for scholarships, and be at least a little more selective about which jobs I took on. I wouldn't have to worry about what might happen to us if I ever got sick or injured or couldn't work."

Chance dropped his grip on her, stepped back. "But you would have been selling your soul had you done that."

"I make compromises all the time."

"Not like that, you don't."

THE TRUTH WAS, Chance thought irritably, Molly had no idea how cold and ruthless some of the truly wealthy could be, and he didn't want her to ever know. Not firsthand, anyway. She'd come close enough to finding out in her dealings with the vaulted Worthington Academy.

"I'm asking you not to be naive," he said again.

Molly angled her thumb at the center of her

chest. "And I'm asking you to consider my position." The soft swell of her breasts rose and fell. "To imagine what it is like to not have that fallback of security that comes from family money and connection."

She rushed on, giving him no chance to interrupt, "Because if I did have that, Chance, I wouldn't have to work so hard to build my business."

Her lips pinched together stubbornly. "Or meet Babs tomorrow. Never mind leave everything and everyone I know behind and move to Dallas. But I don't have that luxury, Chance, and odds are, I never will. The most I can do is earn as much money as possible as quickly as possible and provide for my son."

She had a point, he acknowledged silently. For a lot of reasons she wasn't as secure financially as she wanted to be at this point in her life, and given how hard she worked, she should be.

She was also his woman—whether she admitted it yet or not. He was her man. Yes, he had acted on her son's behalf, but he hadn't done nearly enough to protect *her* feelings or keep *her* safe. That would change. Effective immediately. "Let me go with you tomorrow," he said.

She moved away from the mantel. "I don't need your protection."

Except she did. He caught up with her as she retrieved her shoes. Tried again. "Molly…"

She perched on the edge of his sofa and slipped on her heels, then stood. "If you understand nothing else, understand this. I have to move forward and do this the way I always have. On my own."

MOLLY HAD PLENTY of time to regret the abrupt way she'd left Chance's ranch the evening before and returned to her home in town. The truth was she hadn't been nearly as irritated with him as she was with herself.

The womanly side of her kept telling her she was making a mistake in not allowing Chance to stand by her side or run interference for her.

Whereas the independent single mom told her it would be a mistake to rely on anyone other than herself, lest she upend the life she had already built for herself and her son.

As for the romantic part of her?

Well, she knew what that required.

A long-term future with Chance.

But was that even realistic, knowing how he felt about everything that mattered to her? The first of which was earning enough money to obtain real financial security.

Molly had no answer. What she did know was the meeting with Babs could be the key to a lot of things. Hence she had to go. Even if it meant disappointing Chance.

So Molly dressed in her most elegant business suit, the one she reserved for premiere networking events, grabbed her briefcase and headed out to Lake Laramie.

Two cars were already in the drive. A sleek white Mercedes and a minivan with a Realtor sign on the side. She walked up to the fixer-upper, one of many year-round rentals at the lake. It had an artificial wreath on the door and a sparsely decorated small Christmas tree inside. The Realtor, whose daughter attended Braden's preschool, said hello to Molly, then turned back to Babs. "I'll wait to hear from you."

"You'll have an answer on the property by noon," Babs promised.

The Realtor left them to discuss possible renovations. Molly turned to Babs, her attitude professional. "How much were you thinking of doing?"

Babs laid a silk scarf over the worn sofa, then perched on it. "Actually, I'd like to sit and talk first."

Getting better acquainted might help break the ice, but something felt off. Ignoring her growing sense of unease, Molly sat opposite her.

Babs smiled. "I understand you have a son, Braden, and that he was recently wait-listed at Worthington Academy."

Molly's alarm deepened, but she kept her outward cool. "How do you know that?"

"I do background checks on all prospective business associates. As it turns out, Worthington Academy recently did one on you."

Molly had agreed to a credit check as part of the application process. It was standard at most businesses requiring a long-term payment commitment.

She hadn't expected such information to become available to anyone but school officials.

But if Babs had had her investigated, it would have shown up. The same way all the details of her life had shown up when Aaron's family had her life scrutinized by a PI.

Molly felt as punched in the gut now as she had then.

Seeming to realize she'd caught Molly off guard, Babs continued haughtily, "The school wants to know who the parents of their prospective students are. Delia attended WA, and I've maintained my connections there, to help business associates, so I made a few calls to see how the process was going."

Without my knowledge or consent? That was unacceptable.

But wary of insulting a person she still hoped to get work from at the end of the day, Molly merely smiled. "I don't understand what my son's education has to do with this job."

"I still have pull at Worthington. I can get him off the wait list before Christmas."

That would be nice. Had it been merit—not connection—based. Doing her best to appear as if this sort of thing happened to her every day, Molly asked calmly, "Why would you want to do that?"

"Oh, honey." Babs shook her head at Molly. "It wouldn't be without quid pro quo. You'd do a favor for me. I want you to help me shake some sense into my daughter once and for all."

Molly's insides twisted with anxiety. Chance had said she had blinders on...

Babs frowned. "She's been mooning after that

ne'er-do-well cowboy for years now. Lamenting their breakup to the point she won't date respectable beaux more than once or twice. And then only if forced."

Molly could see why that would not make for a happy situation. For anyone. "Again…" A hint of steel entered her tone. "What does this have to do with me?"

Babs waved a dissolute hand. "Delia, as you know, does not like to chase lost causes. She needs to see that Chance has indisputably moved on. With you. And the most dramatic, lasting impression way for that to happen is for her to catch you with him, in flagrante."

This was getting surreal. Molly felt the room sway. "You're…joking."

Babs opened her handbag. "I assure you I am not. Now, Chance will be here in about ten minutes. If not sooner, given the message I left for him just shortly before you arrived. Delia will be here ten minutes after that."

Babs fished her keys from her bag. "All you

have to do is seduce Chance in plain view, right here in the living room, and you will not only have more work than you can handle in Dallas but your son will be admitted to Worthington Academy, his tuition for the next five years fully paid in advance."

The proposition was so outrageous it took her a moment to recover. "I don't know why you think I would even consider something so preposterous."

"Let's not play games, Molly."

"I'm not," Molly gritted out.

Babs's expression turned ugly. "You had no qualms asking Chance Lockhart to pay for Braden's interview at Worthington Academy."

Sure she hadn't heard right, Molly blinked. "What are you talking about?"

Babs smirked, as if she still held the high card. "You didn't know? How sweet." She leaned closer, telling Molly snidely, "The problem is, as usual, Chance was a little too cheap. It would have taken a much larger donation to secure a spot for Braden at semester. Fortunately, I am prepared to spare no expense, if it means getting my daughter to start taking advantage of her own good fortune with Mr. X." Babs stood and shrugged on her mink coat. "So you see, Molly, you and I have that in common. We're both willing to do whatever it takes to safeguard our children."

Shock reverberated through her. "But I'm nothing like you!" Molly insisted.

Babs flashed a manipulative smile. "Aren't you? We will see. You have approximately six minutes to decide..."

CHANCE PASSED BABS on the road leading to the lake house. She was driving with her usual cool confidence. Which made him wonder what had happened with Molly.

Molly's red SUV was in the driveway.

He walked in. She was on the sofa, her head in her hands.

"Molly?"

She looked up, her complexion ashen.

Damning himself for ever letting her make this venture alone, he crossed quickly to her side. He knelt in front of her, consoling her the best he could under the circumstances. "What happened here?"

Molly stared at him, a thousand emotions shimmering in her eyes. Anger, hurt, resentment. Disbelief…

"What in hell did Babs say to you?" Clasping Molly's hands, he pulled her to her feet. She moved woodenly into his embrace.

He wrapped his arms around her. Instead of melting against him the way she usually did, she pulled away.

"Chance, no!" she said in a strangled voice, looking all the more upset and betrayed. "I don't want—" She choked up, shaking her head. "We can't…"

Aware he'd never seen her more devastated, he threaded his hands through her hair and lifted her face to his.

Beneath her confusion, a glimmer of need shone in her eyes. "Molly," he said again as his head lowered to hers. Desperate to comfort her in any way he could, he touched his lips to hers just as the front door opened behind them.

"Really," Delia's low voice rang out in the chilly room. "You don't have to put on a show just for me. I already know what Mother's scheme is."

That was good, Chance thought. Because he sure as hell didn't.

Chapter Fourteen

Molly could see why Delia was upset. She lifted her hands. "I didn't agree to help your mother with her sleazy machinations."

Delia took off her sunglasses, her demeanor as world-weary as her tone.

"And yet here you are in Chance's arms," the heiress observed, as if she couldn't bear yet another disappointment.

Chance frowned. "I initiated that. Molly wasn't cooperating." Looking irritated to find himself being a third wheel in whatever was going on, he turned his level glance back to Molly. "Is this why?"

Figuring he was going to find out eventually, Molly folded her arms in front of her. Chance had been right. She never should have come here today, no matter how lucrative the job or how coveted the connection. Sometimes a job just wasn't worth it. "Babs offered to get Braden accepted at Worthington Academy, his tuition paid for the next five years, if I would be caught in flagrante with you!"

Chance did a double take. "What the *hell*?"

Delia nodded, her shoulders hunched in defeat. "Mother's determined to show me that Chance and I are still all wrong for each other. What she refuses to accept is that we've been over for years now."

Molly wanted to believe that. Just as she wanted to believe that the difference between her background and Chance's would not keep them apart. "Babs thinks you still have feelings for him."

Delia scoffed, "Of course I do! I'll always care about you, Chance. Even though things ended badly. We knew each other too long and too well for me *not* to care for you."

Chance exhaled wearily. "Seeing you again has shown me the same thing."

Delia slid her sunglasses on top of her head. She loosened the belt on her black trench and perched on the edge of the sofa. "But coming all the way out here, going through the offer process with you, finding out how you still feel about monetary success, has also shown me that Mother was right to break us up. I never would have been happy living on a ranch named Bullhaven out in the middle of nowhere, with all those big, smelly Black Angus. Never mind going through the hassle of simultaneously building up two relatively small-time businesses from scratch!"

Molly took umbrage with that. "First of all, Chance's bulls don't smell. I've been around them."

Delia waved off the details. "Maybe not to you. To me, everything out on that ranch is yucky and disgusting. I'm a city girl through and through."

That Molly could see.

The question was…was she?

Was Braden—who loved their small town and Chance's ranch so much—a potential city boy?

Or would her son wish for his roots, the way she was beginning to, and they hadn't even left Laramie County yet!

Her expression sober, Delia continued, "Being dragged out here—repeatedly—on what was clearly a lost cause, also made me realize I don't want to work in the family business anymore, even as second in command. I really hate my mother's maneuverings and all the drama."

"What do you want to do?" Chance asked his ex kindly.

Delia gestured haphazardly, her elitist attitude coming to the fore once again. "Honestly? No clue. Thanks to the trust fund my daddy left me, however, I don't have to be in any hurry to find out."

Molly had always wanted to have that particular option. Now, studying Delia's self-indulgent expression, she wasn't so sure that was such a good thing.

"So maybe you should just tell your mother all that," Molly proposed.

"So she'll leave Molly and Braden alone," Chance added protectively.

"And you." Molly turned back to him.

Once again, just like that, they were a team. At least for the moment.

Delia scoffed. "First of all, talking to my mother, telling her what's in your heart never works. She thinks the world revolves around cold hard cash." Delia paused to let her words sink in. "And Mother's right, for people like us, who have grown up with the world as their oyster, it really does. Which is why I've decided to take Mr. X up on his offer to rescue me from all this and fly back to San Francisco with him."

Suddenly Molly realized why Chance was so concerned about Delia. She'd obviously been sheltered to a fault. And hence, she'd remained incredibly naive despite her overall sophistication. "Are you sure you want to do that?" Molly asked gently. *Be used like that? Like I once was? By a rich man who, at the end of the day, only cares about his own happiness?*

Delia paused to look at Chance, who remained stone-faced, then turned back to Molly. "Mr. X and I have been straight with each other. He wants a beautiful woman on his arm, one who's very good at playing hard to get, to enhance the reputation he wants to build as a ladies' man. So he can up his game."

Game, Molly thought. *How appropriate.*

"And I need a break from my mother's constant haranguing—which Mr. X has agreed to give—by hinting he wants to marry me. Mother won't do anything to interfere with possible billions coming my way," Delia continued.

They all knew that to be true.

"Anyway," Delia finished with an airy shrug as Chance moved closer to Molly and slipped his arm around her waist. "If you want me to tell Mother you carried through on your end of the bargain and got caught in a passionate clinch with Chance so you'll go ahead and get what you need regarding your son's school, I'm happy to do so."

The knowledge Delia felt Molly could be part of any scheme, never mind one that low-down, rankled. His grasp on her tightening, Chance looked equally ticked off by the intimation.

Her fury rising yet again, Molly reminded Delia, "Except I didn't set you up deliberately." She had been trying to do just the opposite.

"Who cares?" Delia moved gracefully to her feet, suddenly looking very much like her mother. "Mother deserves to get scammed the way she was trying to scam me!"

Molly knew revenge was a dish best *not ever* served. "Thanks," she said tightly. "But Braden and I are fine." In fact, this whole episode gave her second thoughts about trying to enroll her son with other children of the very elite. "I'd just as soon not have your mother's involvement."

Delia sighed. "I hear you. Comes with way too many strings." She said her goodbyes. The door closed behind her.

Chance turned to Molly. "I'm sorry you got dragged into the middle of all this."

Molly thought of all that had gone on behind her back.

All she and Chance still had left to discuss.

She stepped away from his warm, comforting embrace, then said, with a deep soul-wrenching bitterness that surprised even her, "You know what, Chance Lockhart? You really should be."

CHANCE COULD TELL by the quietly seething way Molly was looking at him that she was accusing him of something. And just when he thought, especially now that Babs and Delia and Mr. X were out of the way, that he and Molly were ready to take that next big step. "Did I do something?"

"Maybe you should tell me." When he said nothing immediately, her brow arched. "Unless there's *more* than one thing?"

There was only one mistake, and he saw now it had been a big one. He swore fiercely to himself, aware he should have leveled with her way before now. "You found out I intervened on Braden's behalf at Worthington Academy to see he at least got an interview."

"Well, you must not have given enough, because he didn't get accepted."

He resisted the urge to haul her into his arms and kiss some sense into her only because he didn't want hot sex being the only thing keeping them together. "Is that what this is about? You wanted me to buy his way in, the way Babs bartered? Instead of just asking that he be tested and interviewed and given a fair shot?" He studied Molly in confusion. "Because I could still do that," he said carefully.

She tossed her head, her silky auburn curls swirling around her pretty face. Edging closer, she glared at him as if it were taking every ounce of self-control she had for her not to slug him on the chin. "No, you moron! It's about the fact that you found it necessary to buy his pre-admission interview and consideration at all, never mind behind my back!"

He set his jaw. "How do you think my four siblings and I all got in there? How do you think the academy got such an over-the-top campus and facilities without charging six-figure tuition for each and every student? Parents make *huge* donations to pave the way for their kids and if necessary keep them there. It's just the way things are done at that echelon, Molly."

She inhaled deeply, her luscious breasts lifting beneath the sophisticated evergreen business suit. "I see that now." She raked her teeth across the plumpness of her lower lip. "What I don't see is why you didn't explain all that to me a whole lot earlier."

That part, at least, was easy, Chance thought. He returned her frustrated glare. "Because if I had told you that you needed more than just a letter from Sage, another alumni, to boost consideration chances, that you needed a big fat check of at least five figures just to get an interview there, you wouldn't have allowed me to help. And I knew if you were ever going to understand what you were truly asking, in attempting to move to Dallas so Braden could enroll at Worthington Academy or another place just like it, was if you and he experienced it firsthand."

Hurt shimmered in her pretty amber eyes. "You figured I would think it wasn't for him."

Another trap.

"I didn't know how you'd react, frankly. Because, yes, there are a lot of good things about the school, if you subtract the greased wheels and social hierarchy and all that."

"But you didn't think Braden would belong."

Chance stood, legs braced apart, shoulders back, hands on his waist. "He loves bulls, Molly.

Loves his cowboy boots. And his hat. And his friends here. Which isn't to say he wouldn't love a uniform, too. But, yeah, I hoped when the decision finally had to be made that you would want to stay in Laramie and leave him in the school he is in right now." Exhaling roughly, he raked a hand through his hair. "Not because it's going to in any way further enhance or detract from his opportunities, academically or any other way, but because he is *happy* there, and if you ask me, *that*'s what school should be about, making a kid feel happy and confident!" Damned if he didn't suddenly sound like a parent. And an incredibly caring and overprotective one at that.

"I agree."

Chance blinked. Almost afraid to think they might be on the same page once again.

Molly shook her head, her mouth taking on a troubled tilt. "I've been reconsidering my education goals for Braden for days now. Ever since I Skyped with the academy administrators and had that uncomfortable meeting about why he didn't get accepted. And then came back here and saw his Christmas program at the preschool."

Chance moved closer. He cupped her shoulders gently. "If you were having second thoughts, why didn't you tell me?" So they could have talked about it. So he could have confessed what he had already done, and why, and had her understand.

She whirled, sending a drift of perfume heading his way. "Because I hadn't made up my mind entirely! And I didn't want to say anything before I had."

He felt like he were facing off with a bear with his paw caught in a trap. "And now?"

"I've decided to stay in Laramie through the rest of the school year."

That didn't have the permanence he yearned for. Yet, wary of pushing her too hard too fast again and ending up pushing her away, he asked quietly, "What about the two jobs you already have set up in Dallas?"

Regret glimmered briefly in her gaze. She seemed to think she had failed on some level.

He wanted to tell her she hadn't.

He didn't think she would want to hear that, either.

So he remained silent.

With a sigh, she pointed out, her dejectedness more chilling than her earlier anger, "As you said, they are small tasks. And if we put our crews together, we could easily get them done in a couple of weeks. I just wouldn't take on any more out of Laramie County for the time being."

"Well, that's great news," he said, beginning to think she was holding out for the same long-term future he was. In fact, the best Christmas present ever. "To have us working together again."

She didn't seem to think so.

She squared her slender shoulders. "But that doesn't eliminate my need to build up a heck of a lot more of a financial safety net." She looked all the more conflicted. "So I'm still going to eventually have to—"

He held up a hand before she could continue. Grasped her hand before she could move even farther away. "I don't want you and Braden to ever have to want for anything, either," he told her huskily, tightening his fingers on hers. He paused to look deep into her eyes. "And you were right, merging our businesses into one would only bring you in another ten or fifteen percent annual revenue. Nothing close to what you're trying to do moving to Dallas and entering that much more lucrative market."

Her eyes were steady, but her lower lip trembled. "I'm glad you understand that," she said quietly.

"I do. And that," he said with a burst of excitement, "brings me to your Christmas gift." Ignoring the skeptical expression on her face, he led her to the sofa. Sure everything was finally going to work out, he sat down next to her.

Reaching into his jacket pocket, he pulled out a red envelope with her name on it. Handed it to her with a flourish. "Open it!"

She reacted as if he had given her a time bomb instead of a gift. Lips tightening in distress, she protested, "But…it's not Christmas yet. I haven't even gotten you your gift."

Like he cared what she gave him, if she let him fully into her and her son's life, the way he desperately wanted to be. He regarded her steadily. "I want you to have this now," he told her solemnly, giving her hands another gentle squeeze. "So you'll feel better right away."

Still holding his gaze, Molly drew a deep breath, some of her usual good cheer returning. "Well, now I'm curious…"

She eased open the seal. Unfolded the contract. Read quietly. Blinked once and then again. She stared at him uncomprehendingly. "You're gifting me half ownership of Mistletoe?" She narrowed her eyes as if it couldn't possibly be true.

Heart filling with all he felt for her, he confirmed, "And Braden will get half ownership in Mistletoe Jr." Imagining the little tyke's reaction, Chance grinned. "So he actually will have all his wishes come true and get a Leo and Lizzie train set and a real live bull for Christmas. Which, of course, will be kept at Bullhaven Ranch."

The pages detailing the gift fluttered to her lap. One hand splayed across her heart. "This is crazy," she gasped.

"It's what you and Braden deserve," he said. And so much more!

Molly thrust the papers back at him. Pushing him aside with one arm, she shot to her feet. "Chance, you can't do this on a whim!"

"I'm not." It hurt that she would even think that.

Her delicate brow arched.

"I've been thinking about it for days," he rushed to confess. "Wanting to do it." Just not sure how…

She stared at him, clearly not believing a word he said. "You never share interest in your bulls or co-own them with anybody!"

"Until now," he admitted. "You're right. I haven't."

Expression grim, she snatched up the gift notification and waved it in front of his face. "This is worth—"

"Millions, yes." If that didn't prove his devotion to her and to Braden, what would?

Molly swallowed, tears filling her eyes. "And it's completely one-sided," she said as if he had just plotted to utterly destroy her, heart and soul. Instead of make her feel as safe and secure as she had always wanted to be. "You're giving me a ton of revenue."

Including stud fees and endorsements for the retired Mistletoe? Potential winnings for Mistletoe Jr.? He nodded. "Six figures annually, easy." Enough to make relocating herself and her son completely unnecessary. Starting now.

Molly's chin quivered. "And I'm giving you nothing in return."

Okay, maybe he should have considered how the ultra-independent and self-reliant Molly would feel about any one-sided arrangement.

He could still fix this.

"I wouldn't say that." He attempted a joke to lighten the mood. "I wouldn't mind, say, a life-time supply of breakfast *stollen* or homemade German pastries and cookies."

She shook her head. "Chance, this is too much. It's way too much. It's—" Her voice caught on a small sob. She gulped, unable to go on.

Oh, God, he'd hurt her. Which was the last thing he wanted. He pulled her into his arms. Abruptly feeling like his whole life was on the line, he buried his face in the softness of her hair. "The best Christmas gift I could think of to give you."

Her slender body hunched in defeat. "Just like with the Leo and Lizzie train set," she recol-lected sadly.

He knew he'd gone way overboard there. Maybe here, too. But they had fixed that. And they could fix this, too, if she gave him half a chance. "I care about you and Braden." He let her go long enough to get down on one knee, take both her hands in his. "And if this is what it takes to persuade you to stay in Laramie County, then…" His voice got rusty.

"Wow." Molly shook her head, still looking completely shell-shocked, and something else he couldn't identify. Something really treacherous. Her low voice was taut as a string on a violin. "I don't know what to say." She disengaged their hands.

Trying not to read too much into her stiff posture, he rose. Leaning down, he massaged the tense muscles of her shoulders and whispered in her ear, "How about yes?"

"Braden's daddy wanted to pay us to go away." Her voice rich with irony, she placed both her hands on his chest and shoved him away. "Now you're trying to pay us to stay!"

She shook her head, tears flowing from her eyes. "What's that saying?" she asked as if something inside her had been broken irrevocably. Staring at him, she lifted her chin. "The rich really are different?"

Her words stung. He was not the one here with a cash register for a heart. "You act like I'm trying to insult you," he fired back just as angrily.

Amber eyes narrowed. "Aren't you?"

Gut tightening, he stepped back. Aware that the thought of a life without her and Braden was more than he could bear, he reminded her, "You're the one who's always said what you really want is that big financial safety net so you'll never have to worry." He paused to let the weight of his words, the sheer enormity of his gift, sink in. He spoke slowly and deliberately, so if she thought about it long and hard enough, she would understand this was a gift from the heart, pure and simple. *"I'm giving you that."* He was offering to extend his family and merge it with hers. There was no greater gift.

She nodded, her expression maddeningly inscrutable. "Because, as you've said before, money means nothing to you."

"Well, you can't take it with you." Once again, his attempt to lighten the mood with a joke fell flat. He tried again. "You know money doesn't mean anything to me."

"Except it does mean something to you, Chance, just in a very different way." Her low voice trembled with emotion. "For you, it's the freedom to do what you want, when you want, how you want. Without ever having to worry about it."

He shrugged, not about to argue that. "I agree. It's a means to an end."

"Something that allows you to buy whatever you want and or need? Like, say, me?"

He would never be that coarse and manipulative. And if she thought that…did she really know him at all? Did they know *each other*? His frustration rising, he bit out, "I'm not asking you to be my mistress, Molly."

To his surprise, she looked even more betrayed. "Don't you get it, Chance?" Her voice was as flat and final as the look in her eyes. "I wouldn't accept a gift like this from you even if I were your wife!"

Clearly, Chance noted, that was something not about to happen, either. Unless he miraculously managed to fix things.

He spread his hands wide. Tried again. "You're taking this all wrong—"

This time it was she who cut him off with an imperious lift of her hand.

"No, Chance," she reiterated. "I'm not. In fact, I understand *exactly* what you're trying to do here. And that's fix something that can't be fixed by throwing money at it."

He was getting a little tired of being accused of being mercenary when she was the one all about cold hard cash! He glared right back. "There are worse things than searching for a solution, Molly."

"Not like that, not in my view." She steamrolled past, gorgeous ice princess on parade. Her lips pursed. "Which is why this affair has to end."

Another sucker punch to the gut. What little holiday cheer he had in him evaporated completely.

"You're breaking up with me?" he asked, staring at her in disbelief. "Because you didn't like my gift?"

She grabbed her coat and bag and rushed out the door as if her heart were breaking, pausing only to send him one last glance. "You're damn right I am."

Chapter Fifteen

Early on December 24th, Molly put her personal devastation aside, and set out, as per tradition, to deliver her holiday gifts while Braden played with friends. First stop? The beloved Circle H Ranch.

A warm and welcoming look on her face, Lucille ushered Molly into the bunkhouse where the matriarch planned to continue to live until after the holidays. At which point she'd relocate to the recently renovated main ranch house. She accepted the festive platter of German holiday cookies. "Did you bake all these?"

With Chance's help.

But that had been when he'd been at her home almost nightly. Now that seemed unlikely to ever happen again.

A fact Braden was lamenting, too.

Her son hadn't stopped asking for Cowboy Chance.

And Chance was keeping his distance. Going so far as secreting the Leo and Lizzie train set over to Molly's house via his little sister, Sage. So it would be there for her to wrap and Braden to receive "from Santa" Christmas morning, as planned.

Had things turned out otherwise, had Chance not shown her how different they were and always would be, he would have been there, too.

Sharing in the joy. Making the three of them feel like family.

Pushing away the dreams of what might have been, Molly smiled at his mother. "I wanted to say thank you for all you've done for me and for Braden over the last year," she said sincerely.

Lucille responded with a warm hug. "It was my pleasure. And now I have something for you!" She brought something from her desk. "Here is the list of people who've contacted me since the Open House about you doing some work for them."

Molly looked at the printout containing twenty names. She forced a wry smile. "Who says Christmas can't come early?"

Lucille beamed as proudly as if she had been Molly's mother. "Women in my circle like to re-decorate yearly, and thanks to the work you did at the ranch house, they all want you."

Molly was pleased with the results. She could not, however, take full credit. "It wasn't just me and my contractors. Chance and his craftsmen put in a lot of effort, too."

Lucille poured Molly a cup of coffee and ges-tured for her to have a seat at the long plank table. "The two of you make a really good team."

A lump rose in Molly's throat. "We did."

Lucille brought cream and sugar to the table. She sat down. "So it's over?"

So over. Yet even as she thought it, it sounded so final. Too final...

Her heart aching, Molly wiped at a tear spilling down her cheek. Had he only understood her. But he hadn't. "He tried to bribe me into staying here in Laramie."

Lucille frowned. "That was wrong. What you do with your future should be your decision. Period."

The irony was Molly had just about decided to stay in Laramie, not just until summer but permanently. Would have, had Chance not shown her what he really thought of her. Although she supposed at least some of that was her fault, since up to now she had based all her life goals on the premise of one day earning more money and securing a very healthy nest egg to fall back on.

"You have to do what is right for you and your son," Lucille continued, patting the back of

Molly's hand. She drew back and looked in her eyes, advising gently, "Just don't let your pride stand in the way."

Pride? Could that be all it was? Molly hesitated. Ready to partake of the older woman's wisdom, she asked, "What do you mean?"

Lucille ran her hand over the rim of her coffee cup. "When my late husband and I dreamed up the Lockhart Foundation, I am ashamed to admit, it was as much about increasing the stellar reputation of our family as the good works we planned to do with all our accumulated wealth."

Molly paused. "That doesn't sound like you."

Lucille exhaled in regret. "Maybe not now, but I've learned some hard lessons along the way."

Molly guessed Lucille was referring to the financial scandal with the foundation the previous summer that had since been resolved.

Lucille fingered the pearls at her neck. "Although I'd sat on many boards, I'd never actually run a nonprofit."

Molly sipped her coffee. "And that was a problem?"

Grimly, Lucille recollected, "From the very beginning, I realized I was in over my head, but I'd made such a big deal about being the CEO, and I knew it was what Frank had envisioned for my future before he died, so I stayed on the wrong path for much longer than I should have. Because I didn't want to admit I'd made the wrong decision."

Like she was making a mistake now? Molly wondered uneasily.

"Don't let your understandable anger with Chance now rob you of the long-term security that you crave."

Aware Lucille was the closest thing she'd had to a mother in a very long time, Molly fought back the tears clogging her throat. "You think I should stay in Laramie?" *In the community where I grew up, with all my friends? And, like it or not, the man who still turns my heart inside out with just a glance?*

Tenderly, Lucille shook her head. "Only you can intuit what is right for you and Braden, Molly. Just know that if you find yourself headed in the wrong direction, like I once was, that U-turns are not just allowed—they're recommended."

ON THE MORNING OF Christmas Eve, Chance sat in his kitchen, looking at the set of legal papers he had tried to give Molly before she had shown him the door.

Slowly, he unwrapped the last tiny bit of Christmas *stollen* he'd stored in his fridge and took a bite. Once fragrant, soft and delicious, it was now hard, dry and…still delicious. Like a yuletide biscotti.

He sighed, swallowing the last bite he'd been—up till now—unable to part with. Maybe because he had known in his heart that he and Molly would never work out the way he wanted.

Would it have made a difference if he'd told her how he felt about her and Braden, before he'd shown her the legal papers he had hoped would create their family and cement their future?

He didn't know.

Now, would never know...

Outside, he heard the sound of multiple vehicles. Doors slamming. Footsteps coming across his porch.

Grimacing—because he had an idea who this was—he rose and went to answer the insistent knock on his door.

All four of his siblings stood on the porch. Including Zane, his youngest brother, a Special Ops soldier who was usually deployed to parts unknown.

"What happened to you?" Chance gave Zane a hug. Glad to see he was all in one piece, even if Zane did sport a fading bruise across his jaw, and a thick bandage encompassed his left hand.

"The usual," Zane replied cheerfully, looking happy to be home in time for Christmas—something that had almost never happened since he had enlisted.

"You could tell me, but then you'd have to…" Chance mimed a knockout, finishing the age-old combat joke.

"Sounds like I might need to do that anyway," Zane said, hugging him fiercely, before striding in. "What were you thinking? Giving your woman two live bulls for Christmas!"

"They weren't her only Christmas gift!" Chance retorted. He'd had something even better and more romantic planned for that. Not that he'd ever gotten an opportunity to give that present to her.

Wyatt followed, still in ranch clothes. "Just an enticement?"

Chance threw up his hands. "I was trying to give her a reason to stay here in Laramie County, where she belongs."

Garrett strolled in, too. Now happily married himself, he seemed to be the resident expert on domestic bliss. He prodded, "Just not the right reason?"

Chance exhaled in exasperation. "Molly's never made any secret of the fact she wants real financial security for herself and her son. Big-time connections. She could have had all that with me." Even if social climbing was definitely not his thing.

"Just not what every woman wants most of all," Sage murmured, shutting the door behind them.

"And what is that?" Chance asked in frustration. What was everyone seeing that he was missing?

"If you don't know the answer," she scoffed, "you're more clueless than any of us thought!"

Silence fell all around.

Still on the hot seat, Chance eventually asked Sage, "I'm guessing you organized this?"

His little sister nodded, appearing as ridiculously romantic as ever. "I figured you might not listen to me."

True, Chance thought.

"But with all of us here," she insisted stubbornly, "we might have a chance of getting through to you."

He appreciated the sentiment behind their support, if not their actual interference. Chance folded his arms across his chest. "Thanks, but I don't need help with my love life."

Garrett squinted. "The facts say you do."

Wyatt made himself at home. "Look, Chance, we can all see that Molly is the one for you."

Still favoring his injured hand, Zane eased onto a stool, too. "From what I've heard from Mom, the only one."

Glad his Special Forces brother had made it through whatever calamitous event caused his injuries, Chance asked, "Why isn't Mom here, if this is a family meeting?"

"Because," Garrett said triumphantly, "she's at the Circle H, talking to Molly."

Hope rose within Chance. He knew how much Molly loved and respected his mother. If anyone could get his woman—and he admitted he still considered Molly to be his woman—to reconsider their breakup, it was bound to be the matchmaking Lucille.

He studied the faces of his siblings. "Is Mom having any success?"

Shrugs all around. "No clue. You'll have to meet up with Molly to find that out," Wyatt advised.

"The point is," Sage added, "you have an opportunity to make this Christmas the most memorable one you've ever had, Chance, if you can find it in your heart to stop trying to steer the situation to your advantage. Ignore the shield Molly is hiding behind. And give her what she really wants and needs, most of all."

JUST AFTER EIGHT O'CLOCK Christmas Eve, Molly kissed her sleeping son and eased from his bedroom. She wasn't surprised they'd only been able to get halfway through "Twas the

Night before Christmas." Her son was deliriously excited.

Whereas she knew she still had so much to do to make amends before the holiday ended.

She reached for her phone just as a knock sounded on her front door.

Molly looked through the glass.

Chance?

Heart pounding, she opened the door.

He stood on her doorstep in a sport coat, snowy-white shirt, Santa Claus and Rudolph tie, and jeans. He'd recently showered and shaven. His hair had that mussed, sexy look she loved. But it was the hopeful sparkle in his eyes that got to her the most.

She nodded at his tie. "Glad to see you haven't lost your sense of humor."

The crinkles around his eyes deepened. "I thought you might like it."

She liked more than that.

She liked everything about him.

Especially this. The fact that he knew just when she needed him most and showed up.

Because it was the showing up, it was the being there, that was most important of all.

"Seriously." Chance's voice dropped a sexy notch, his gaze devouring her from head to toe. "I hope it's not too late."

Flushing beneath his tender scrutiny, Molly swung the door open wide and motioned him in. "Actually, your timing is perfect," she whispered, ushering him back to the kitchen, where their voices were least likely to carry. "I just got Braden to sleep." Knowing now was the time to give him a gift from the heart, too, she ignored the shaking of her knees and hurried on. "I've been wanting to talk to you. I don't like the ways things ended the last time we—"

He put a finger to her lips. Hazel eyes serious, he interrupted sternly, "If anyone is going to apologize, it's got to be me."

This she hadn't expected.

Shaking his head ruefully, he took her all the

way into his arms. Threaded one hand through her hair, wrapped the other reverently around her waist. "I'm sorry, Molly. For trying to maneuver you into making the decisions I wanted regarding your future." He hauled in a rough breath, admitting, "My only responsibility as the man in your life is to do everything I can to support you in whatever you want."

Molly splayed her hands across his chest; the rapid beat of his heart matched hers. Tears of happiness misted her eyes as the relief inside her built. "You mean that?"

"I do." He nodded soberly. Then bent to tenderly kiss her brow. "I don't care where we live, Molly, as long as we're together."

She knew what it took for him to concede that. "But Bullhaven..." Her voice broke.

"Can be run with or without me on the premises every day."

"But there's Mistletoe and all the other bulls, not to mention Mistletoe Jr."

He promised gruffly, "I'll work that out, too."

She saw he meant it. With all his heart and soul. Still…"It's your life work."

He nodded. His eyes held hers. "And only part of what I want," he said thickly.

Her heart pounded like a wild thing in her chest. She moved in closer, taking in all the heat and strength he had to give. "What's the rest?" She let her eyes rove his handsome face. Memorizing this Christmas for all time.

He lifted her hand, kissed the back of it and then held it against his chest. Their gazes still locked, he told her, "I want you. And Braden. And a life together." His voice caught as the tears she'd been holding back spilled over her lashes and flooded her cheeks.

"Which is why you tried to give us part ownership in Mistletoe and Mistletoe Jr. Because they are the most precious gifts you have to offer."

He tightened his grip on her. "So you do understand that I only gifted them to you to secure your financial future, and show you how much I wanted us to be family?"

She nodded. "I know how much you love your prize bulls. And that you giving us half owner-ship in them was a very big deal."

"Then why did you take it as an insult?"

"Because the enormity of the gift—the long-lasting deeply personal nature of it—scared me, Chance." She tipped her head back to better see into his eyes. "For years now, I've been tell-ing myself I didn't need anyone, so long as I had enough money to keep Braden and I safe. I thought my duty as his parent was to provide all the material things and opportunity denied me as a child. I couldn't see—didn't want to see—that we already had everything we needed, here in Laramie. A great home. A caring community of friends and neighbors."

Chance drew her close. "A school that fits him and his exuberant, engaging personality."

She leaned into him. "I wanted more for him."

He stroked a hand through her hair. "More for you?"

Molly nodded. "All of it, based on the things that I've since realized matter the least." His strength and tenderness gave her the courage to go on. "And then you came into my life. Challenging everything. Showing me whether I wanted to acknowledge it or not that the grass wasn't always greener and the luxe life was no guarantee of happiness."

She wreathed her arms around his broad shoulders. "And while financial security will always be important, it's not nearly as crucial as having someone to love who will love you back." Her voice trembled with emotion as she took the biggest leap of faith of all. "And I do love you, Chance." Letting him see and feel just how much, she kissed him deeply, sweetly.

"Damn, Molly," Chance kissed her back with all the yearning she had ever wished for. "I love you too," he whispered, kissing her again. "So much…"

Chance released her and got down on one knee. He reached into his pocket. "Which is why I got this…"

Inside the box was a diamond engagement ring. He lifted his face to hers, an endless supply of hope and faith shining in his eyes.

Mirrored in her heart.

He clasped her hand tightly, looking as if this were the most important moment in his life. "Marry me, Molly."

The joyful tears overflowed again. She tugged him to his feet and drew him back into her arms. "On one condition," she promised, holding him so close their hearts pounded in unison. "We stay in Laramie."

Surprise warred with the pleasure and relief on his handsome face. "You're not moving to Dallas?"

She shook her head, kissing him again, tenderly and persuasively. "This is where I want to be, for Christmas and forevermore." She gazed into his eyes. "Right here with you."

Epilogue

One year later...

"Is it time to go yet?" Braden asked. "Can we give the bulls their Christmas presents?"

Molly looked at Chance. It was still half an hour before the appointed feeding time on Christmas Eve, but if they didn't spring into action soon, their little guy was going to burst with excitement. A fact the love of her life seemed to know very well.

Chance grinned. "I think we can go now, buddy."

The three of them donned their hats, coats and gloves and headed out to the barn, a little red wagon full of specialty grain sacks, emblazoned with each bucking bull's name, behind them. One by one, Braden called out a jubilant "Merry Christmas!" to each and every animal. Then, with Chance and Molly's help, he carefully poured the yuletide gifts into the buckets of regular feed before Chance set them in the stalls.

Finally, they made their way to the barn that held the trio of prize-winning cattle.

Seeing them walk in, Mistletoe let out a low bellow. Jr. and Momma followed suit. Both bulls came over to the edge of their pens. Chance hoisted Braden in his arms. As had become custom, Braden gently petted their heads under Chance's supervision, while Molly went over to check on the only female of the bunch. Eventually, Chance and Braden came over, too, their twin sets of cowboy boots echoing on the cement barn floor.

Braden peered through the opening in the metal pen rails. "How come Momma Cow is getting so fat?" He frowned at her sagging, barrel-shaped tummy.

Molly had been wondering when Braden would notice the unmistakable weight gain. "She's going to have another baby bull in the spring."

Braden perked up. "I like babies!" he said.

Molly took a deep breath. "That's good." She and Chance had been waiting for the right time. Maybe this was it. "Because Daddy and I like them, too. So we were thinking," she continued as casually as she could, "that the three of us should have a baby, too." Smiling, Chance telegraphed his support and reached over and squeezed her hand. "Then you'd have a little brother or sister."

Braden tipped his cowboy hat back and thought that over. "Is the baby going to be born in the barn?"

Molly and Chance choked back laughter. Soberly, Chance knelt down. "Probably the hospital," he said.

"Okay." Braden happily considered that, then moved on. "Can we put out the treats for Santa?"

It was a little early yet for that.

On the other hand, they had a Lockhart family party to go to in a little bit, so maybe it was good to do as much as possible now. "Sure," Molly and Chance said, as in tune about this as everything else.

They went inside and washed up. Molly poured a small glass of milk while Braden arranged a selection of treats on a plate, then went to play with his Christmas village and ranch.

As delighted about their expanding family as she, Chance ran his hand possessively over Molly's tummy. Briefly he inclined his head at Braden, murmuring, "That went better than expected."

They hadn't been sure how Braden would take the news. Although they had *hoped*...

The thought of the new life growing inside her filled Molly with warmth. "I think so, too."

She turned to Chance, aware how much had changed in the months since they'd first become involved.

They'd married in July. She'd converted her home in town to an interior design studio and office for their joint general contracting firm. Chance was teaching her and Braden the bucking-bull and ranching business. Best of all, not only was Braden thriving in the school he had always gone to but he was relishing his new "cowboy" life on an actual ranch. And he had the doting daddy she'd always wanted for him, too.

She paused to kiss her ruggedly sexy husband. "Have I told you lately that thanks to you, all my dreams have come true this year?"

All the love she had ever wanted shone in his eyes. "Mine, too," he rasped contentedly.

She hugged him close, aware she had never felt so joyous. "Merry Christmas, cowboy."

Chance stroked a hand through her hair and tenderly kissed the top of her head. "Merry Christmas to you, too, darlin'."

* * * * *

MILLS & BOON®

Why shop at millsandboon.co.uk?

Each year, thousands of romance readers find their perfect read at millsandboon.co.uk. That's because we're passionate about bringing you the very best romantic fiction. Here are some of the advantages of shopping at www.millsandboon.co.uk:

* **Get new books first**—you'll be able to buy your favourite books one month before they hit the shops

* **Get exclusive discounts**—you'll also be able to buy our specially created monthly collections, with up to 50% off the RRP

* **Find your favourite authors**—latest news, interviews and new releases for all your favourite authors and series on our website, plus ideas for what to try next

* **Join in**—once you've bought your favourite books, don't forget to register with us to rate, review and join in the discussions

Visit **www.millsandboon.co.uk**
for all this and more today!